Monica ©

Adventures

Maurício

#3

WHO'S SAYING NASTY THINGS ABOUT ME... ONLINE?!

Charm Z
NEW YORK

Monica

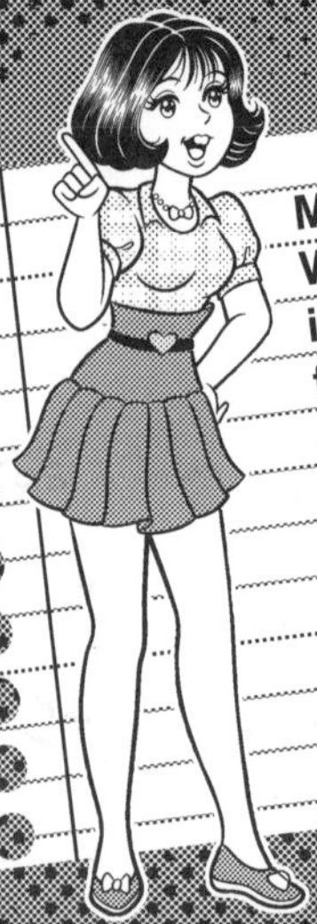

Monica is a sweet, happy, buck-toothed, teenage girl. When she was younger, she was known for being intolerant of disrespect and always stood up for her friends. That is, unless Jimmy-Five and Smudge would cause her trouble, then Monica would bash them with her favorite plush blue bunny, Samson! Still, occasionally, she does her classic bunny bashings as a teen, but has chilled out when it comes to Jimmy-Five, who has been catching her attention a lot more lately. Monica is the leader of the gang because of her honest and charisma-tic—and powerful—personality.

J-Five

Jimmy-Five, or J-Five, has always been picked on for his speech impediment. He used to lisp, which caused him to switch letters around, such as r's for w's, when he would speak. He has grown out of that as a teen, unless he's nervous, which typically happens around a certain girl. He also was picked on because of the five strands of hair he had on his head, which have all sort of filled out as a teen. Still, J-Five is sometimes made fun of for his hair, but he doesn't let it get to him as much anymore! When J-Five was young, he would often try to steal Monica's blue bunny from her and attempt to take over as leader of the gang with his questionable schemes. J-Five is no longer focused on being head of the gang as much as he's focused on being close with his friends, and closer to one friend in particular…

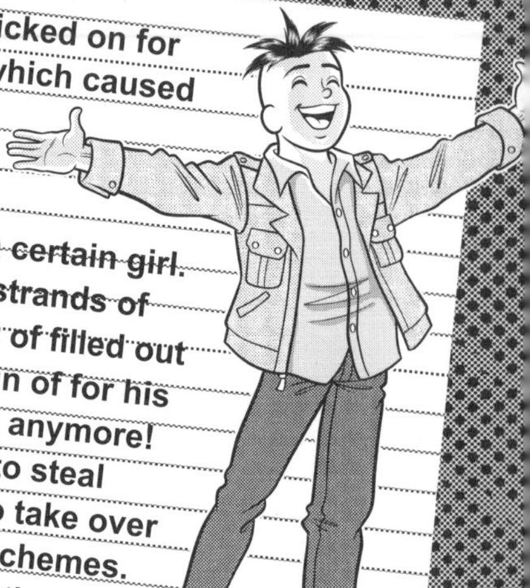

Smudge

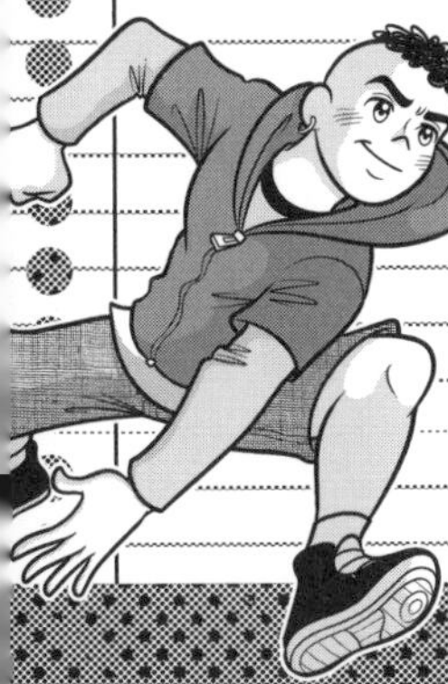

Smudge has never liked water and prefers his messy and dirty lifestyle over showers, rain, swimming, or even drinking water any day, but he's warmed up to taking showers as a teen… sort of. He cleans up sometimes mainly because the opinion of girls has started to matter to him, unlike when he was a kid. Smudge loves sports, especially skateboarding and soccer because of how radical they are. He also loves comics, and shares this love with his best friend, J-Five! Smudge is kind of the "handyman" of the gang, always helping his friends in times of need but typically also messing everything up.

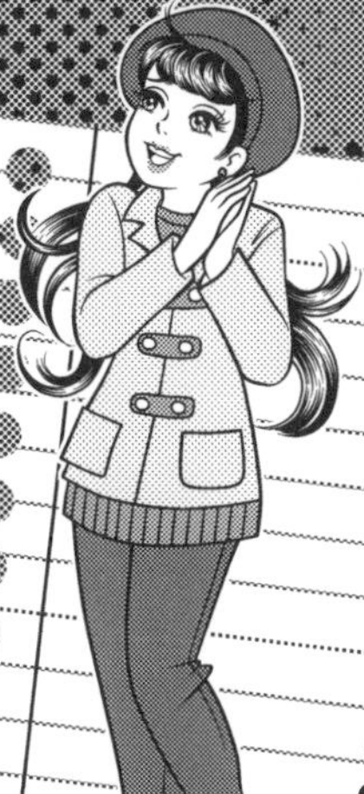

Maggy

Maggy is Monica's best friend, always having her back and being there for her in good times and bad. Maggy is also a huge lover of cats. Maggy has always had a voracious appetite, mostly eating watermelons but never discriminating against any other food put in front of her. Maggy is more conscious of what she eats now… perhaps a little too much. She is virtually obsessed with proper nutrition, sports, and exercise instead of eating anything she sees.

Adventures

#3 "Who's Saying Nasty Things About Me...Online?!"

Characters, Story, and Illustration created by MAURICIO DE SOUSA
ZAZO AGUIAR and WELLINGTON DIAS—Cover Artists
PETRA LEÃO—Script
MARCELO CASSARO and LINO PAES—Pencils
CAROLINE HONDA, CRISTINA H. ANDO, JAIME PODAVIN, PAULO ROBERTO MATHEUS COSTA, RONASA G. VALIM, and TATIANA MONTEIRO—Inks
MARCELO CASSARO—Lettering
MARIA DE FÁTIMA A. CLARO, MARIA APARECIDA RABELLO, and JAE HYUNG WOO—Art Coordination
MAURICIO DE SOUSA, MARINA TAKEDA E SOUSA—Script Supervisors
ALICE K. TAKEDA—Executive Director
SIDNEY GUSMAN—Editorial Planner
WAGNER BONILLA—Art Director
ÍVANA MELLO, SOLANGE M. LEMES—Original editors
PECCAVI TRANSLATIONS—Original Translations
Special thanks to LOURDES GALIANO, GRACIELE PEREIRA, RODRIGO PAIVA, TATIANE COMLOSI, MARINA TAKEDA E SOUSA, MÔNICA SOUSA, and MAURICO DE SOUSA

© 2019 Mauricio de Sousa Editora – All rights reserved.
Originally published as Turma da Mônica Jovem #57 by Panini Comics.
©MSP- Brasil/2013
www.turmadamonica.com.br
All other editorial material ©2019 by Charmz.
All rights reserved.

JEFF WHITMAN—Editor, Production, Dialog Restoration
KARR ANTUNES—Editorial Intern
JIM SALICRUP
Editor-in-Chief

Charmz is an imprint of Papercutz.

PB ISBN: 978-1-5458-0325-7
HC ISBN: 978-1-5458-0324-0

Printed in China
July 2019

Charmz books may be purchased for business or promotional use.
For information on bulk purchases please contact Macmillan Corporate and Premium Sales Department at
(800) 221-7945 x5442

Distributed by Macmillan
First Charmz Printing

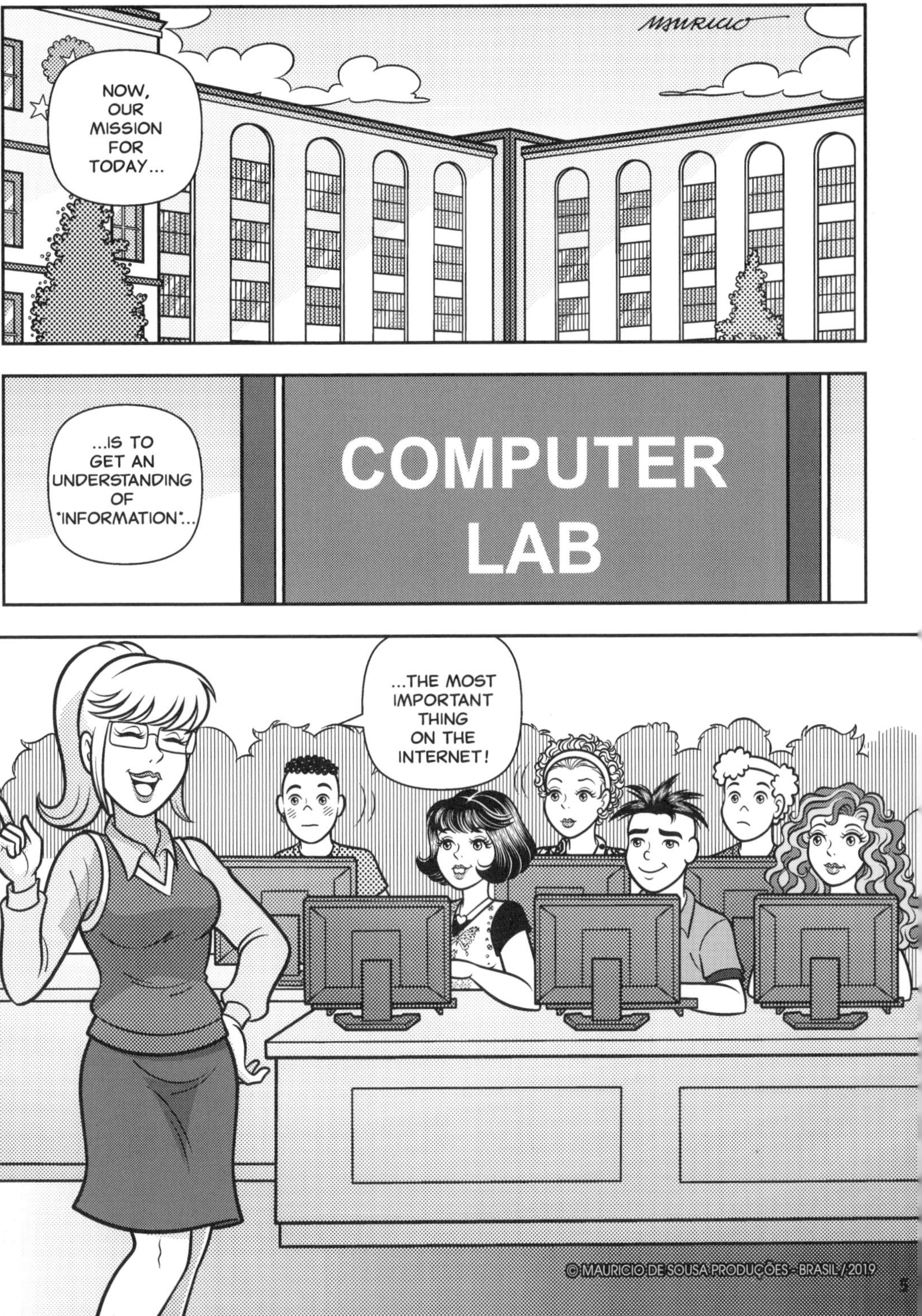
NOW, OUR MISSION FOR TODAY...
...IS TO GET AN UNDERSTANDING OF "INFORMATION"...
COMPUTER LAB
...THE MOST IMPORTANT THING ON THE INTERNET!

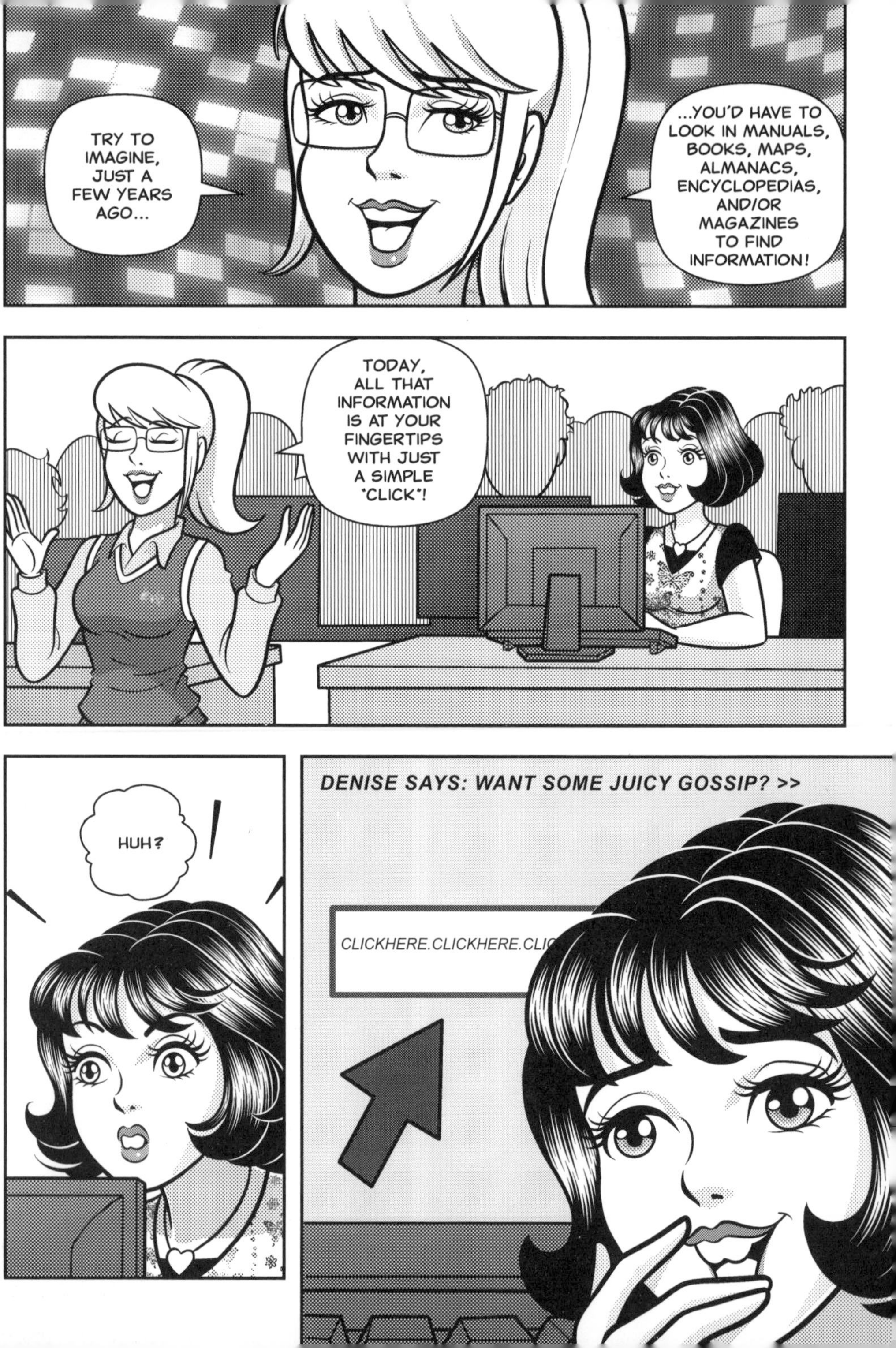
TRY TO IMAGINE, JUST A FEW YEARS AGO...
...YOU'D HAVE TO LOOK IN MANUALS, BOOKS, MAPS, ALMANACS, ENCYCLOPEDIAS, AND/OR MAGAZINES TO FIND INFORMATION!
TODAY, ALL THAT INFORMATION IS AT YOUR FINGERTIPS WITH JUST A SIMPLE "CLICK"!
HUH?
DENISE SAYS: WANT SOME JUICY GOSSIP? >>
CLICKHERE.CLICKHERE.CLIC

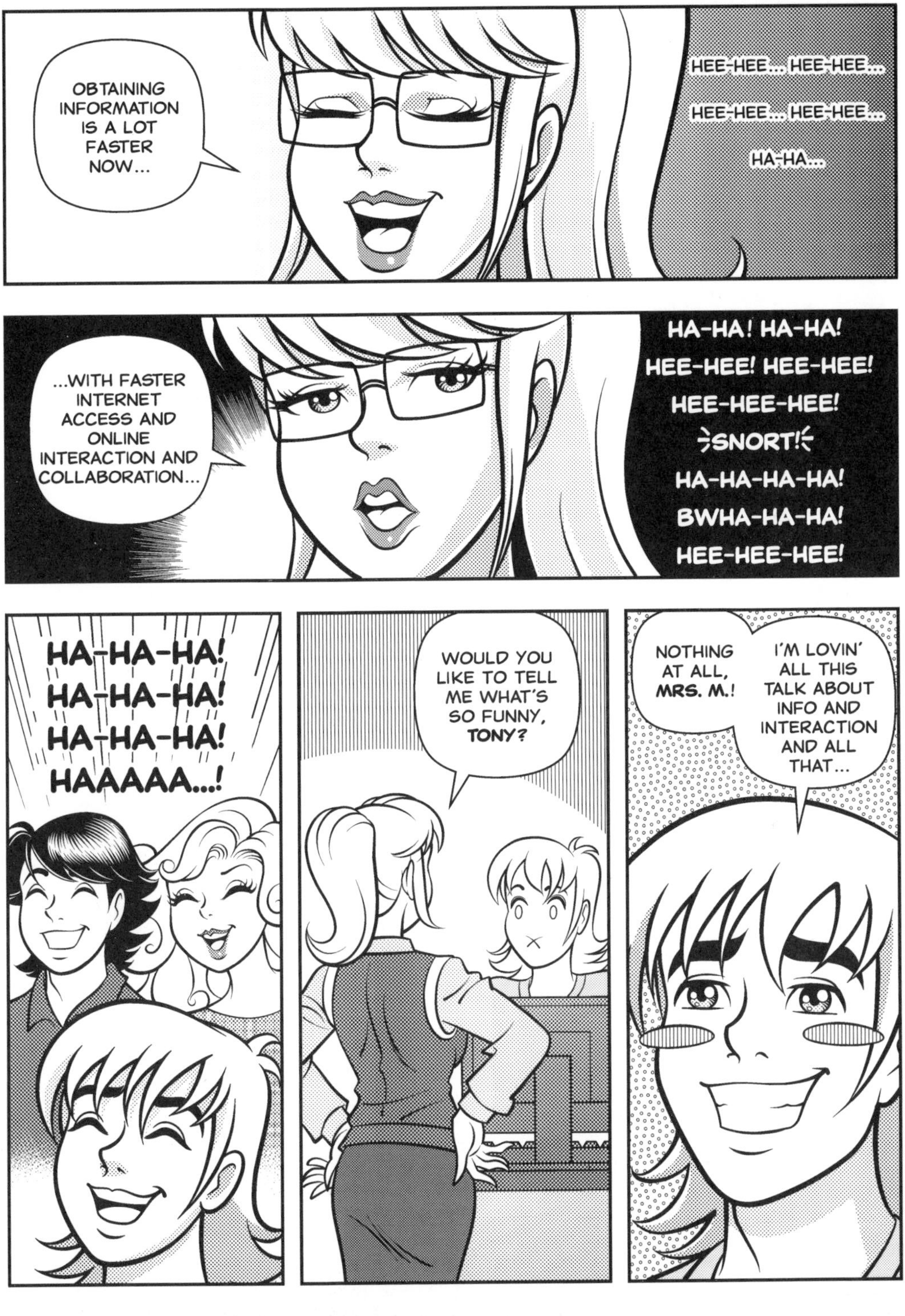

OBTAINING INFORMATION IS A LOT FASTER NOW...
HEE-HEE... HEE-HEE...
HEE-HEE... HEE-HEE...
HA-HA...
...WITH FASTER INTERNET ACCESS AND ONLINE INTERACTION AND COLLABORATION...
HA-HA! HA-HA!
HEE-HEE! HEE-HEE!
HEE-HEE-HEE!
SNORT!
HA-HA-HA-HA!
BWHA-HA-HA!
HEE-HEE-HEE!
HA-HA-HA! HA-HA-HA! HA-HA-HA! HAAAAA...!
WOULD YOU LIKE TO TELL ME WHAT'S SO FUNNY, TONY?
NOTHING AT ALL, MRS. M.!
I'M LOVIN' ALL THIS TALK ABOUT INFO AND INTERACTION AND ALL THAT...

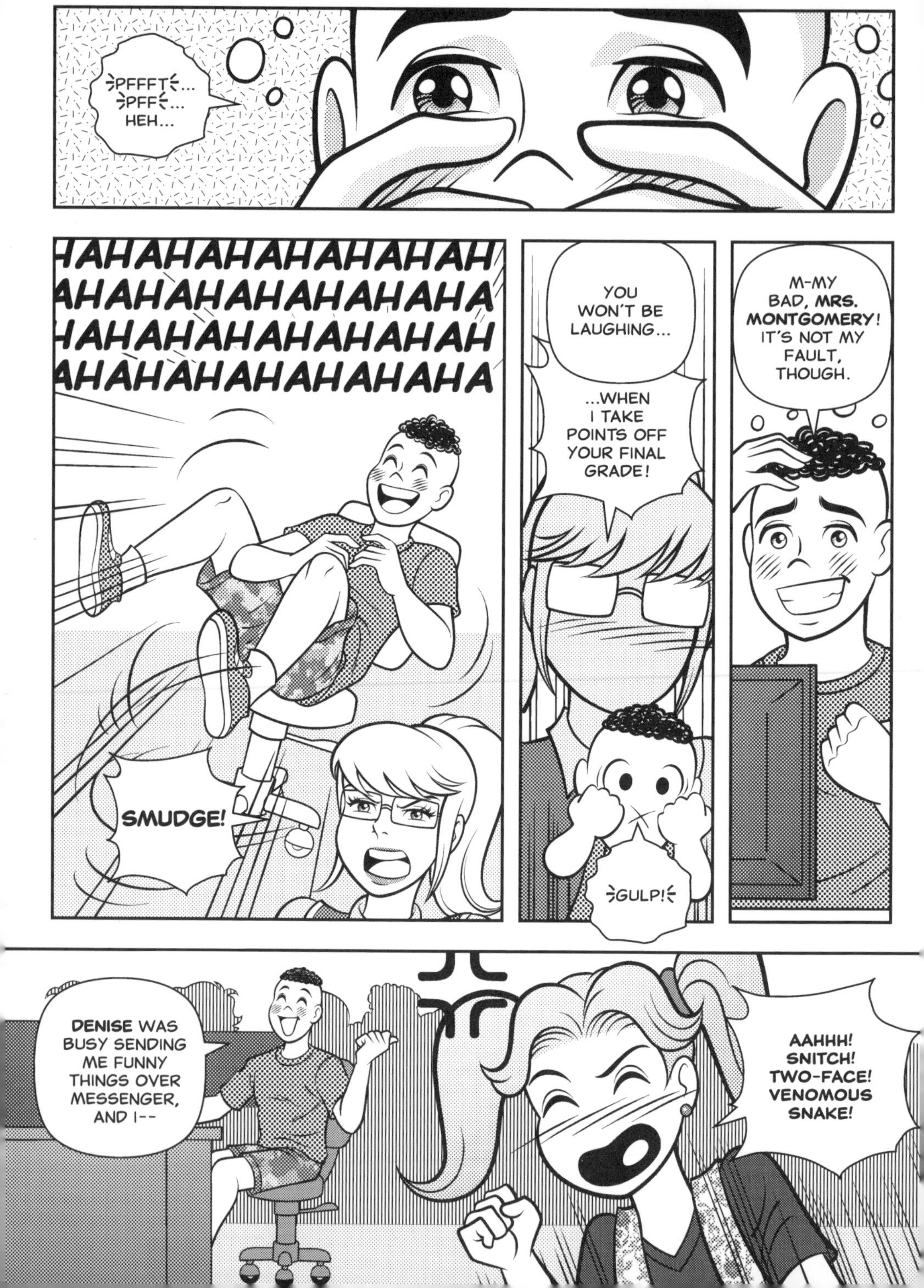
PFFFT... PFF... HEH...
HAHAHAHAHAHAHAHAH AHAHAHAHAHAHAHAHA HAHAHAHAHAHAHAHAH AHAHAHAHAHAHAHAHA
SMUDGE!
YOU WON'T BE LAUGHING...
...WHEN I TAKE POINTS OFF YOUR FINAL GRADE!
GULP!
M-MY BAD, MRS. MONTGOMERY! IT'S NOT MY FAULT, THOUGH.
DENISE WAS BUSY SENDING ME FUNNY THINGS OVER MESSENGER, AND I--
AAHHH! SNITCH! TWO-FACE! VENOMOUS SNAKE!

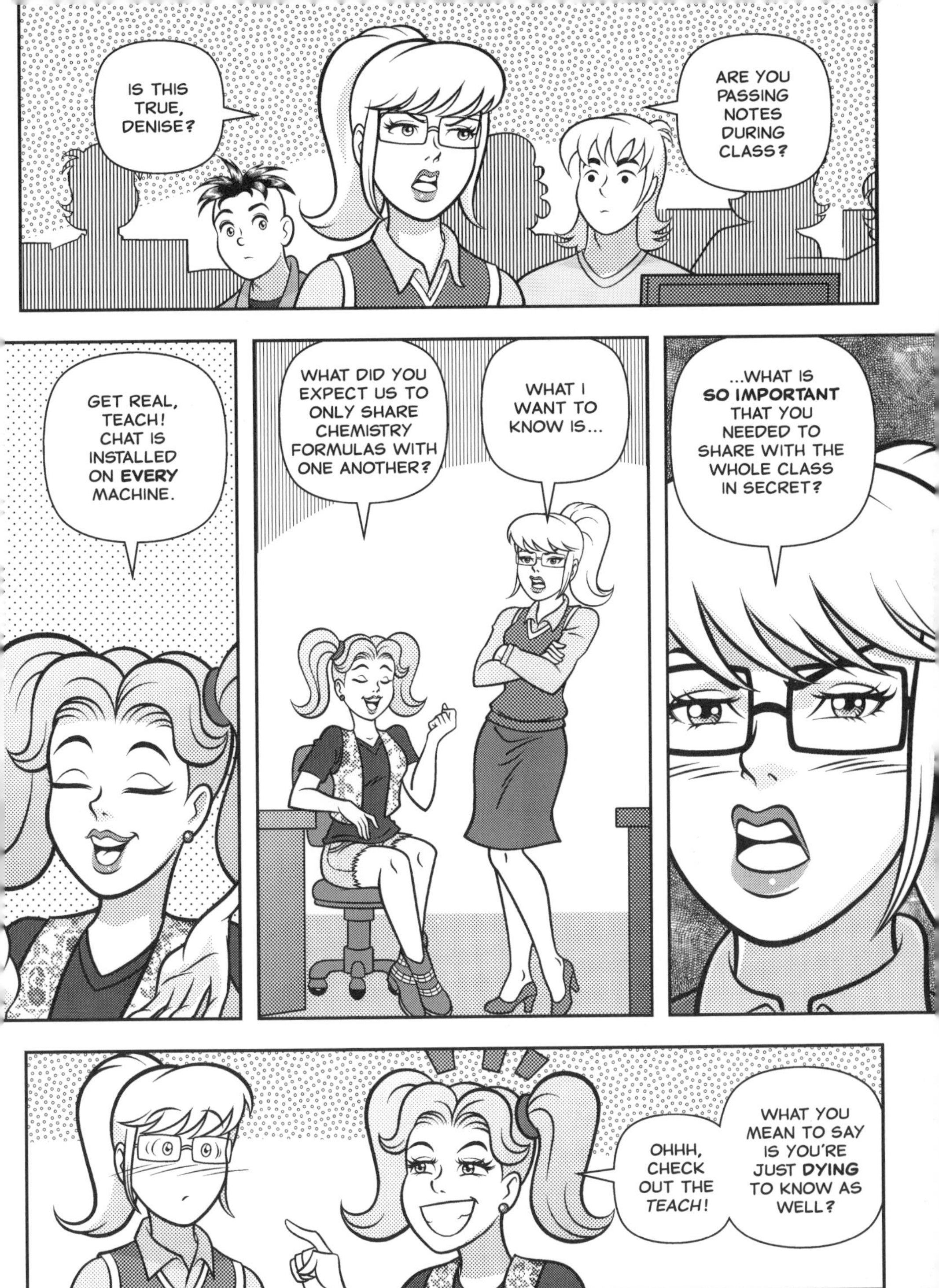
IS THIS TRUE, DENISE?
ARE YOU PASSING NOTES DURING CLASS?
GET REAL, TEACH! CHAT IS INSTALLED ON **EVERY** MACHINE.
WHAT DID YOU EXPECT US TO ONLY SHARE CHEMISTRY FORMULAS WITH ONE ANOTHER?
WHAT I WANT TO KNOW IS...
...WHAT IS **SO IMPORTANT** THAT YOU NEEDED TO SHARE WITH THE WHOLE CLASS IN SECRET?
OHHH, CHECK OUT THE *TEACH*!
WHAT YOU MEAN TO SAY IS YOU'RE JUST **DYING** TO KNOW AS WELL?

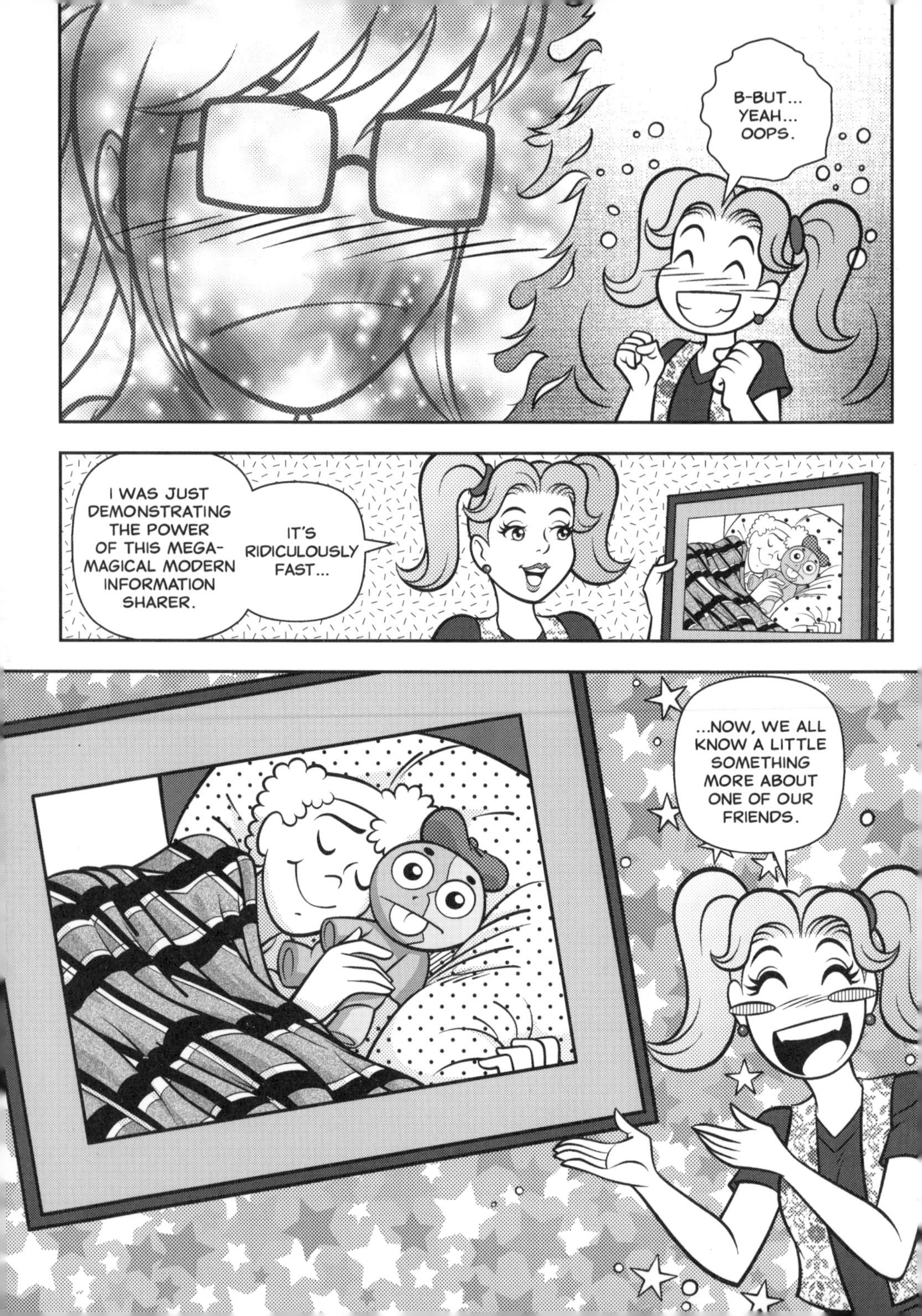
B-BUT... YEAH... OOPS.
I WAS JUST DEMONSTRATING THE POWER OF THIS MEGA-MAGICAL MODERN INFORMATION SHARER.
IT'S RIDICULOUSLY FAST...
...NOW, WE ALL KNOW A LITTLE SOMETHING MORE ABOUT ONE OF OUR FRIENDS.

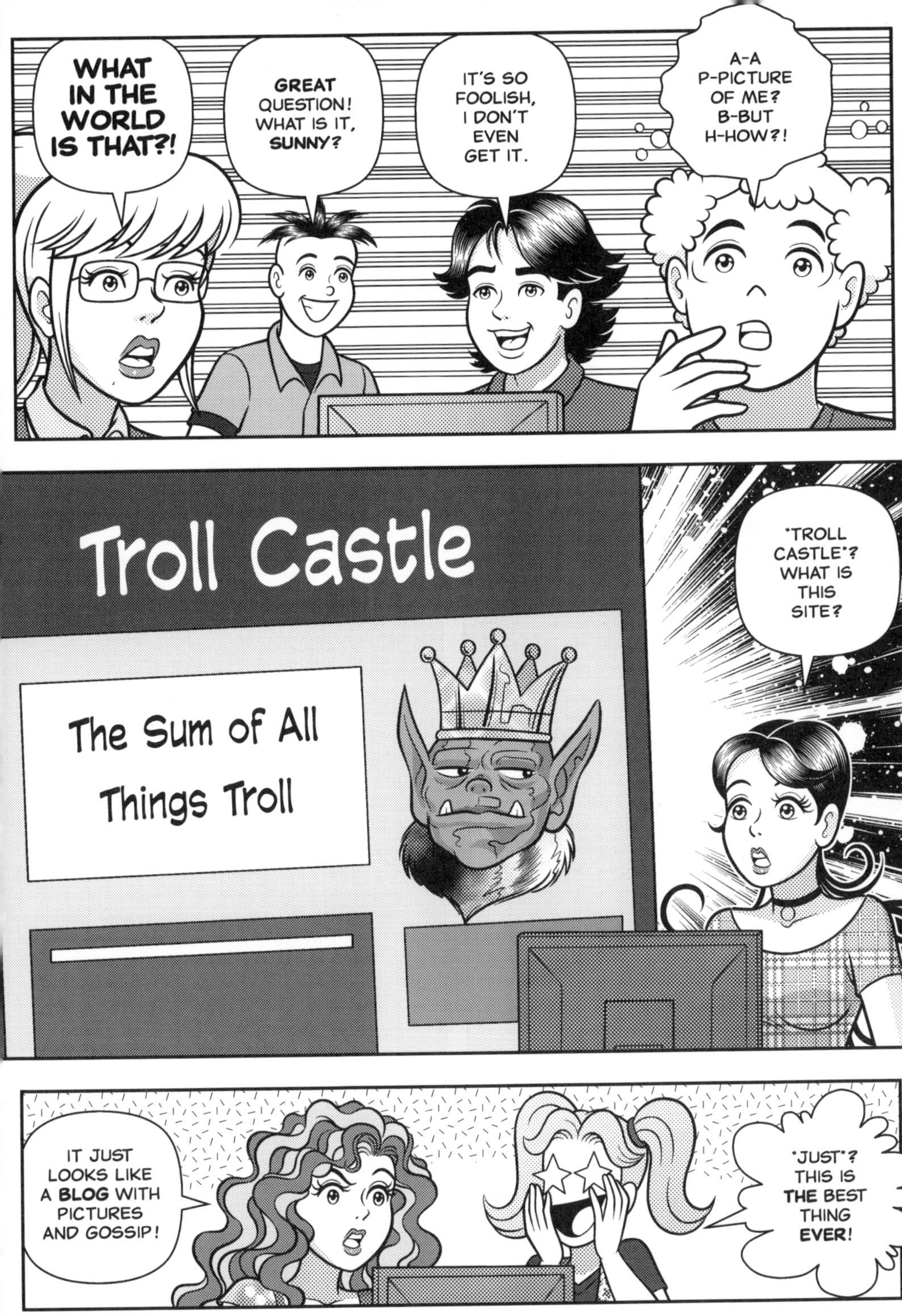
WHAT IN THE WORLD IS THAT?!
GREAT QUESTION! WHAT IS IT, SUNNY?
IT'S SO FOOLISH, I DON'T EVEN GET IT.
A-A P-PICTURE OF ME? B-BUT H-HOW?!
Troll Castle
The Sum of All Things Troll
"TROLL CASTLE"? WHAT IS THIS SITE?
IT JUST LOOKS LIKE A BLOG WITH PICTURES AND GOSSIP!
"JUST"? THIS IS THE BEST THING EVER!

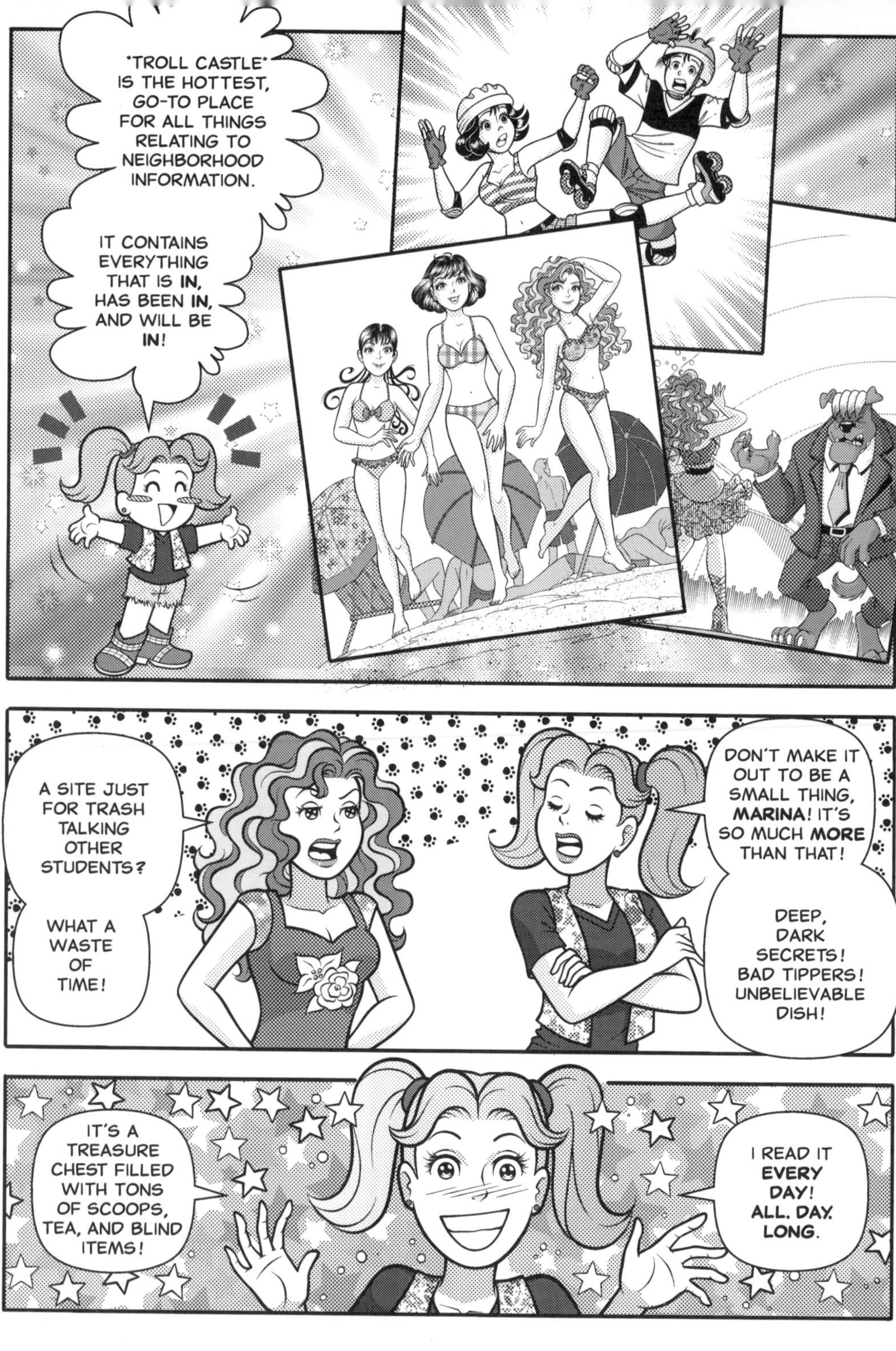

"TROLL CASTLE" IS THE HOTTEST, GO-TO PLACE FOR ALL THINGS RELATING TO NEIGHBORHOOD INFORMATION.
IT CONTAINS EVERYTHING THAT IS **IN**, HAS BEEN **IN**, AND WILL BE **IN**!
A SITE JUST FOR TRASH TALKING OTHER STUDENTS?
WHAT A WASTE OF TIME!
DON'T MAKE IT OUT TO BE A SMALL THING, **MARINA**! IT'S SO MUCH **MORE** THAN THAT!
DEEP, DARK SECRETS! BAD TIPPERS! UNBELIEVABLE DISH!
IT'S A TREASURE CHEST FILLED WITH TONS OF SCOOPS, TEA, AND BLIND ITEMS!
I READ IT **EVERY DAY**! **ALL. DAY. LONG**.

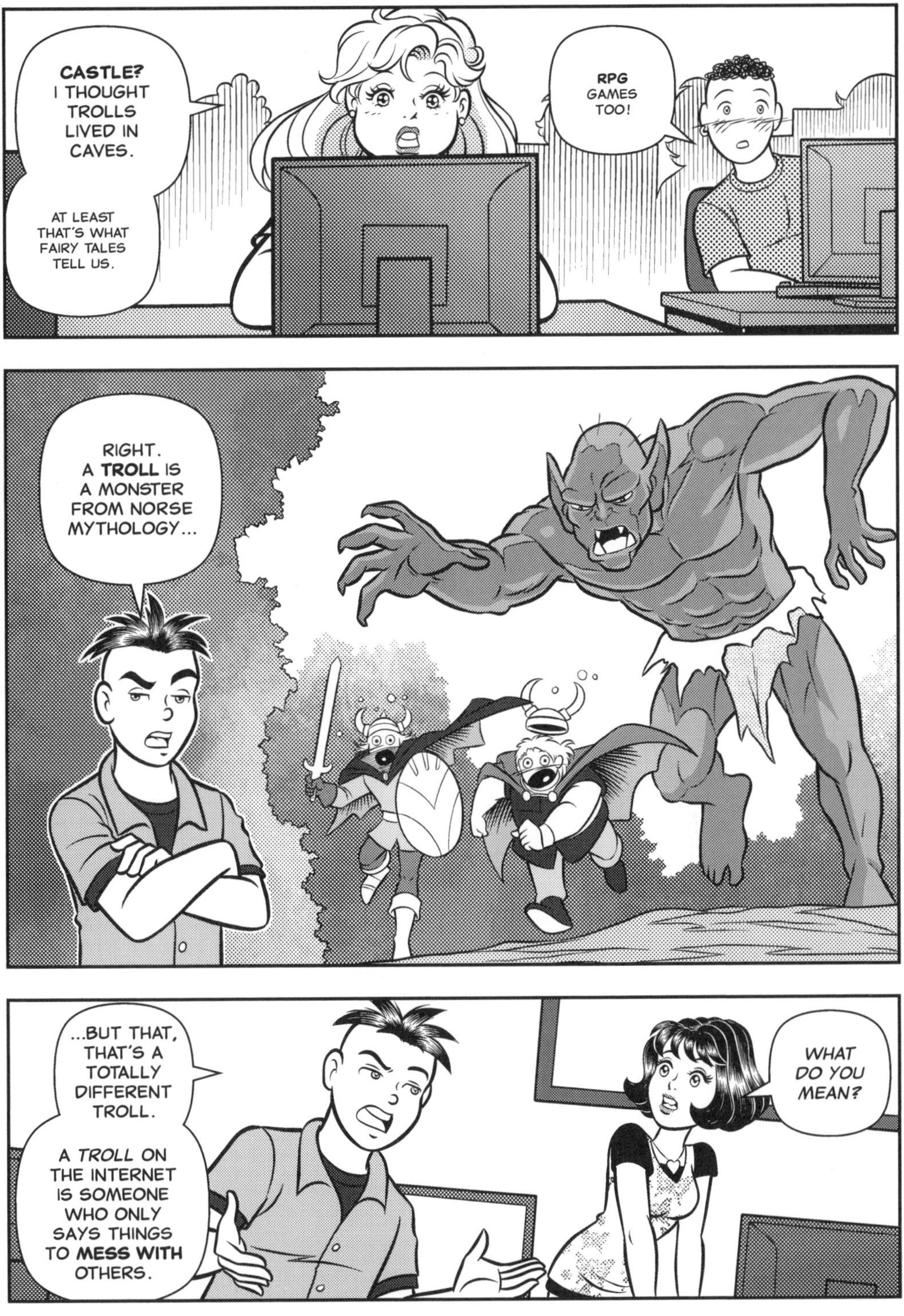
CASTLE? I THOUGHT TROLLS LIVED IN CAVES.
AT LEAST THAT'S WHAT FAIRY TALES TELL US.
RPG GAMES TOO!
RIGHT. A **TROLL** IS A MONSTER FROM NORSE MYTHOLOGY...
...BUT THAT, THAT'S A TOTALLY DIFFERENT TROLL.
A *TROLL* ON THE INTERNET IS SOMEONE WHO ONLY SAYS THINGS TO **MESS WITH** OTHERS.
WHAT DO YOU MEAN?

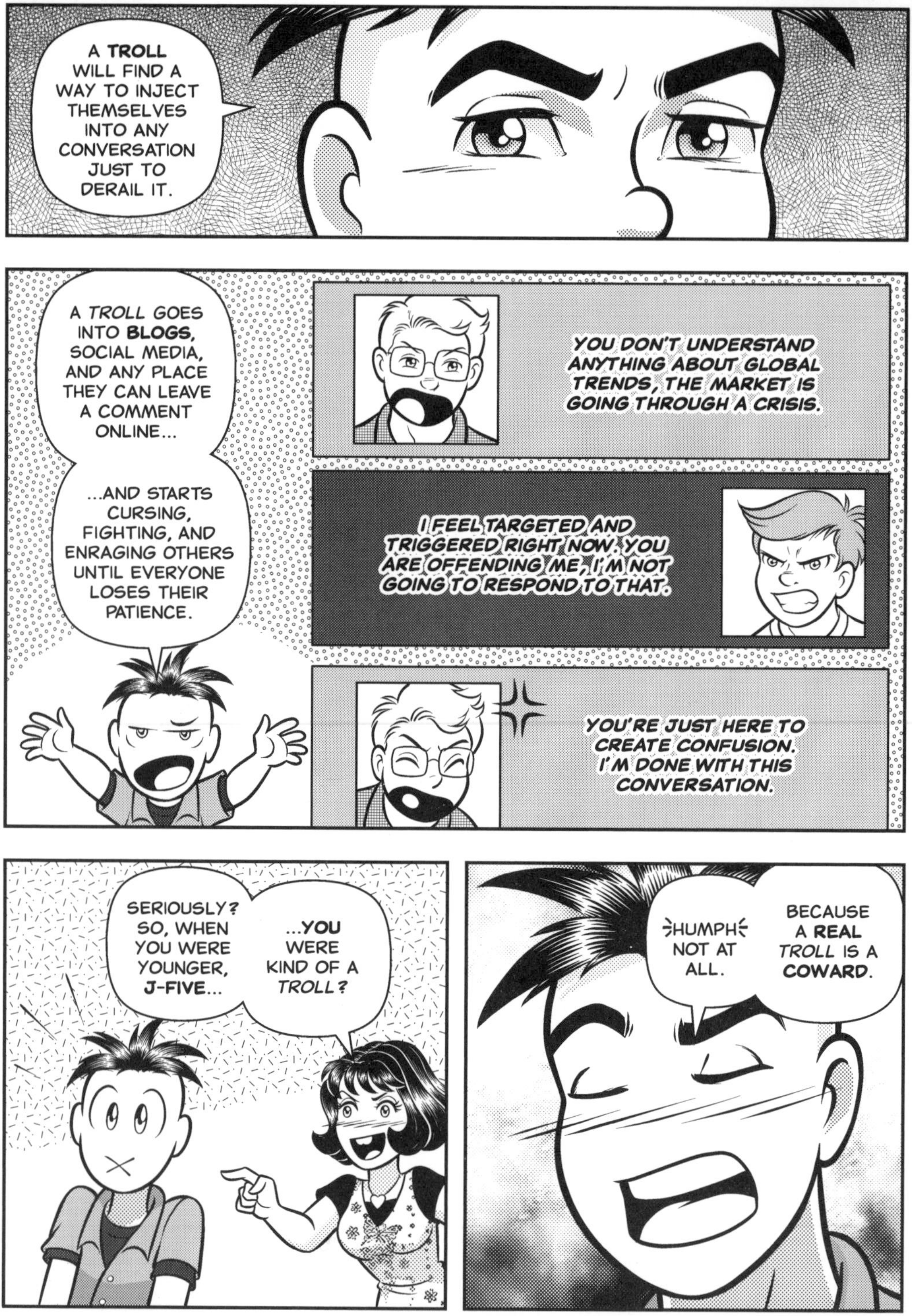
A **TROLL** WILL FIND A WAY TO INJECT THEMSELVES INTO ANY CONVERSATION JUST TO DERAIL IT.
A *TROLL* GOES INTO **BLOGS,** SOCIAL MEDIA, AND ANY PLACE THEY CAN LEAVE A COMMENT ONLINE...
...AND STARTS CURSING, FIGHTING, AND ENRAGING OTHERS UNTIL EVERYONE LOSES THEIR PATIENCE.
YOU DON'T UNDERSTAND ANYTHING ABOUT GLOBAL TRENDS, THE MARKET IS GOING THROUGH A CRISIS.
I FEEL TARGETED AND TRIGGERED RIGHT NOW. YOU ARE OFFENDING ME, I'M NOT GOING TO RESPOND TO THAT.
YOU'RE JUST HERE TO CREATE CONFUSION. I'M DONE WITH THIS CONVERSATION.
SERIOUSLY? SO, WHEN YOU WERE YOUNGER, **J-FIVE**...
...**YOU** WERE KIND OF A *TROLL*?
HUMPH NOT AT ALL.
BECAUSE A **REAL** *TROLL* IS A **COWARD**.

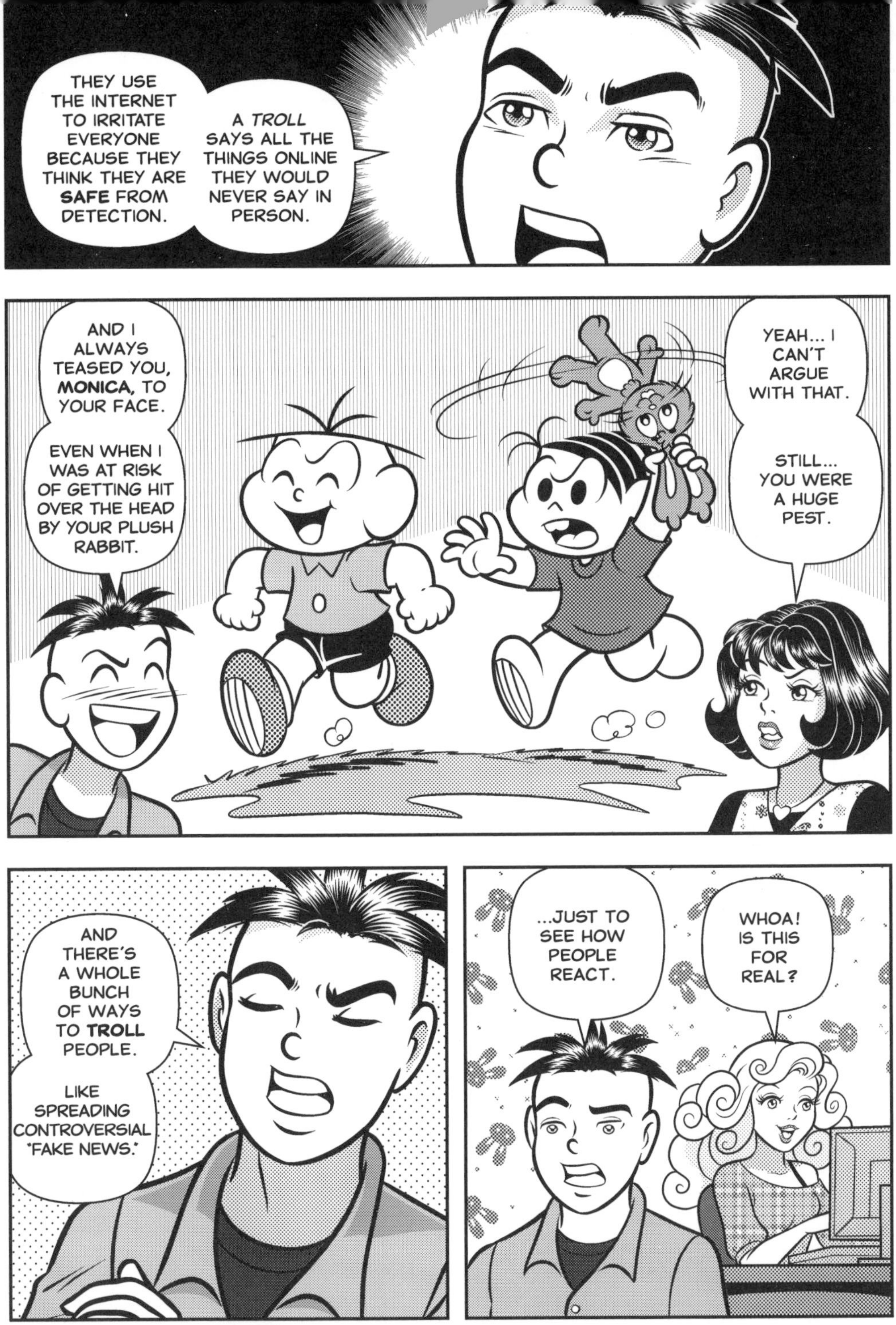
THEY USE THE INTERNET TO IRRITATE EVERYONE BECAUSE THEY THINK THEY ARE SAFE FROM DETECTION.
A TROLL SAYS ALL THE THINGS ONLINE THEY WOULD NEVER SAY IN PERSON.
AND I ALWAYS TEASED YOU, MONICA, TO YOUR FACE.
EVEN WHEN I WAS AT RISK OF GETTING HIT OVER THE HEAD BY YOUR PLUSH RABBIT.
YEAH... I CAN'T ARGUE WITH THAT.
STILL... YOU WERE A HUGE PEST.
AND THERE'S A WHOLE BUNCH OF WAYS TO TROLL PEOPLE.
LIKE SPREADING CONTROVERSIAL "FAKE NEWS."
...JUST TO SEE HOW PEOPLE REACT.
WHOA! IS THIS FOR REAL?

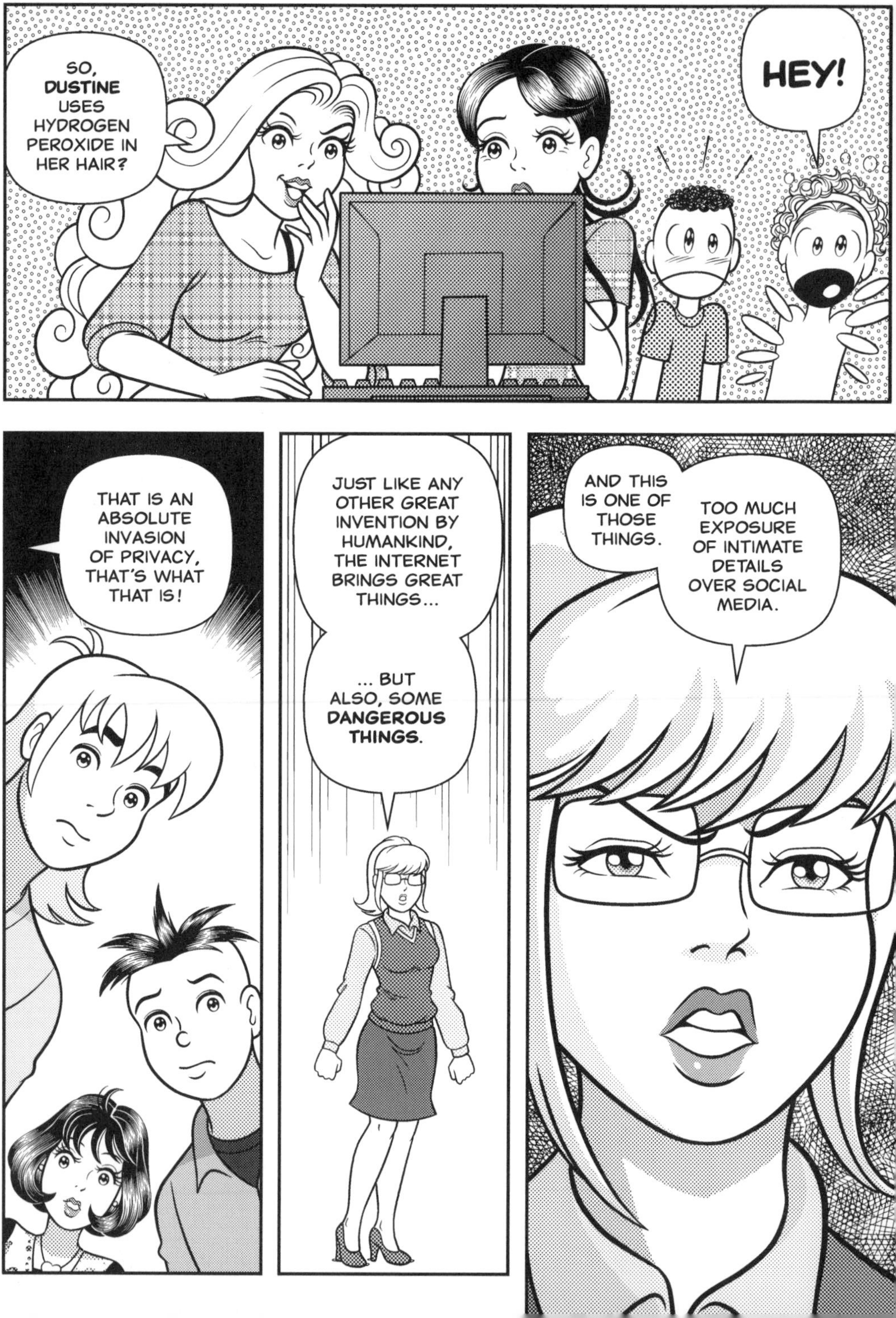
SO, **DUSTINE** USES HYDROGEN PEROXIDE IN HER HAIR?
HEY!
THAT IS AN ABSOLUTE INVASION OF PRIVACY, THAT'S WHAT THAT IS!
JUST LIKE ANY OTHER GREAT INVENTION BY HUMANKIND, THE INTERNET BRINGS GREAT THINGS...
... BUT ALSO, SOME **DANGEROUS THINGS.**
AND THIS IS ONE OF THOSE THINGS.
TOO MUCH EXPOSURE OF INTIMATE DETAILS OVER SOCIAL MEDIA.

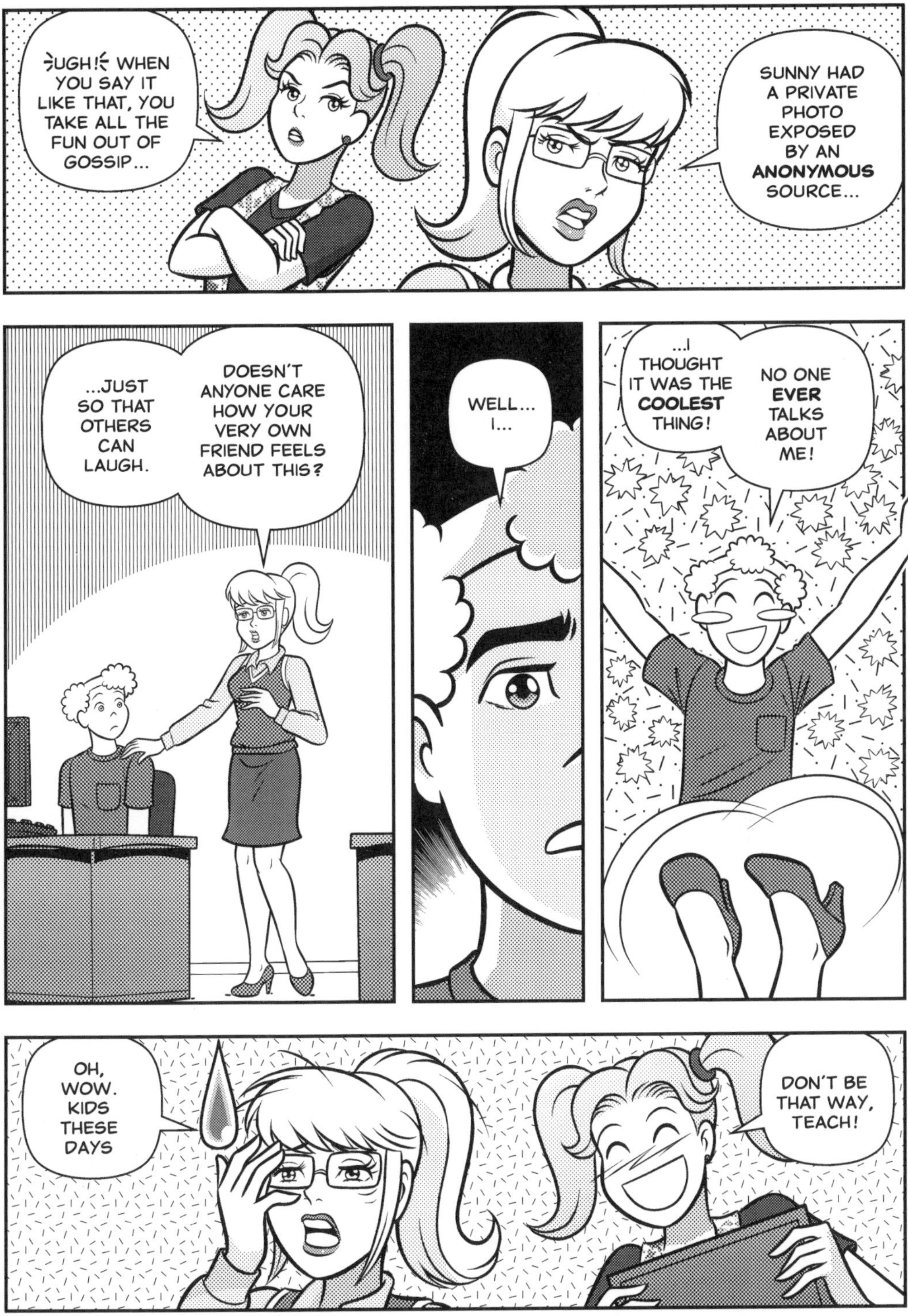
UGH! WHEN YOU SAY IT LIKE THAT, YOU TAKE ALL THE FUN OUT OF GOSSIP...
SUNNY HAD A PRIVATE PHOTO EXPOSED BY AN **ANONYMOUS** SOURCE...
...JUST SO THAT OTHERS CAN LAUGH.
DOESN'T ANYONE CARE HOW YOUR VERY OWN FRIEND FEELS ABOUT THIS?
WELL... I...
...I THOUGHT IT WAS THE **COOLEST** THING!
NO ONE **EVER** TALKS ABOUT ME!
OH, WOW. KIDS THESE DAYS
DON'T BE THAT WAY, TEACH!

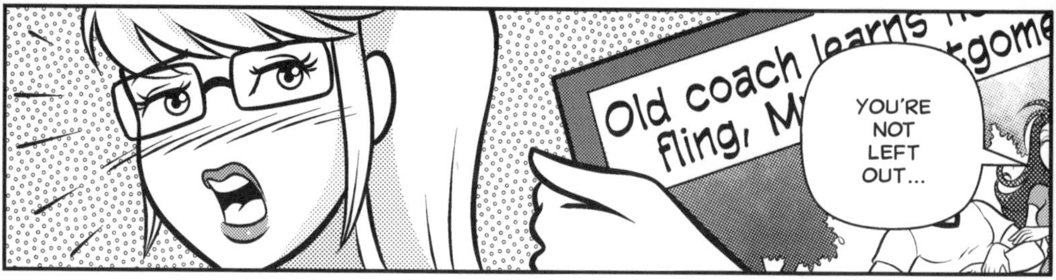
YOU'RE NOT LEFT OUT...

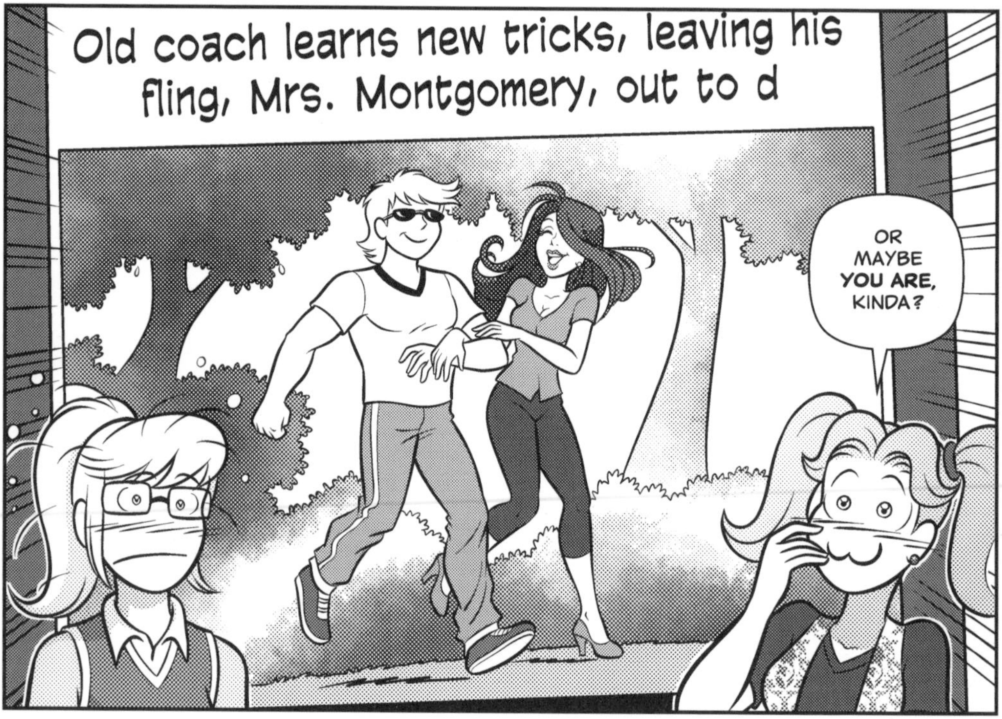
Old coach learns new tricks, leaving his fling, Mrs. Montgomery, out to d
OR MAYBE **YOU ARE,** KINDA?

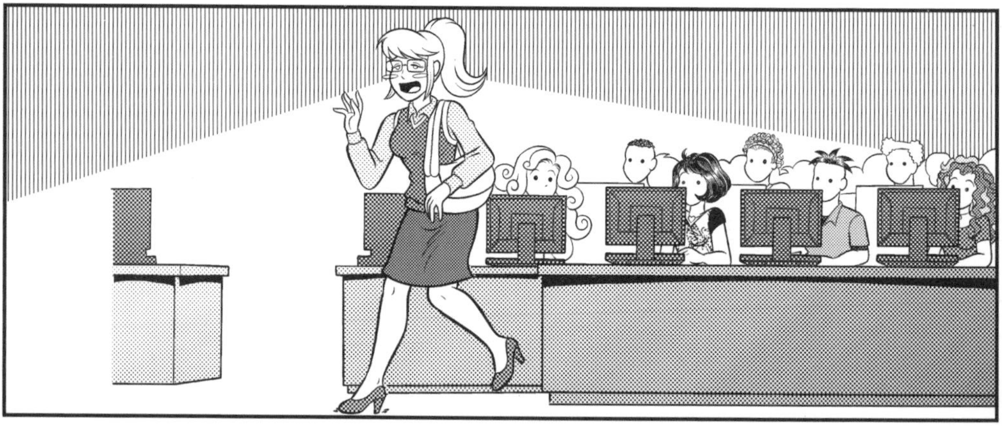

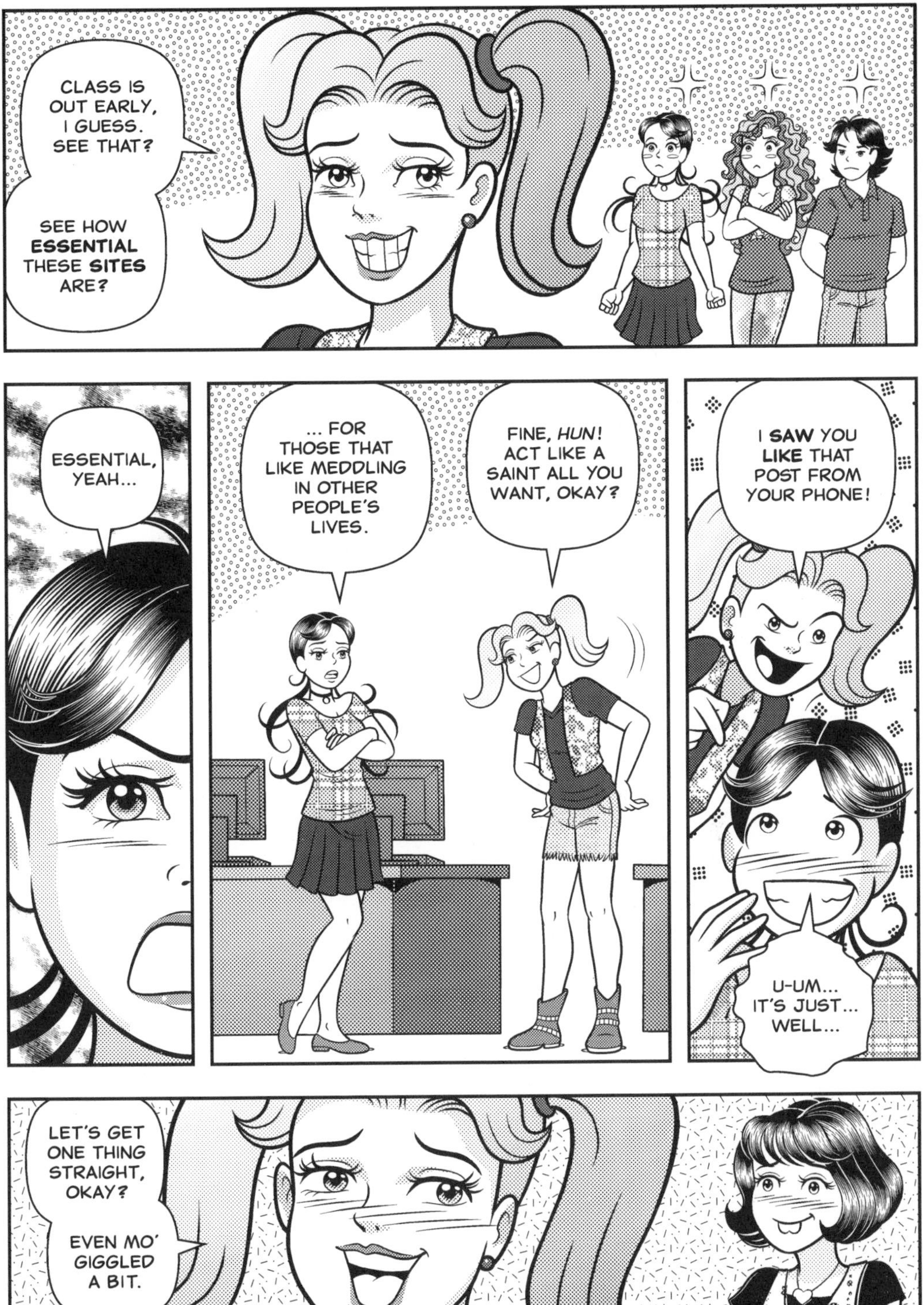

CLASS IS OUT EARLY, I GUESS. SEE THAT?
SEE HOW **ESSENTIAL** THESE **SITES** ARE?
ESSENTIAL, YEAH...
... FOR THOSE THAT LIKE MEDDLING IN OTHER PEOPLE'S LIVES.
FINE, *HUN*! ACT LIKE A SAINT ALL YOU WANT, OKAY?
I **SAW** YOU **LIKE** THAT POST FROM YOUR PHONE!
U-UM... IT'S JUST... WELL...
LET'S GET ONE THING STRAIGHT, OKAY?
EVEN MO' GIGGLED A BIT.

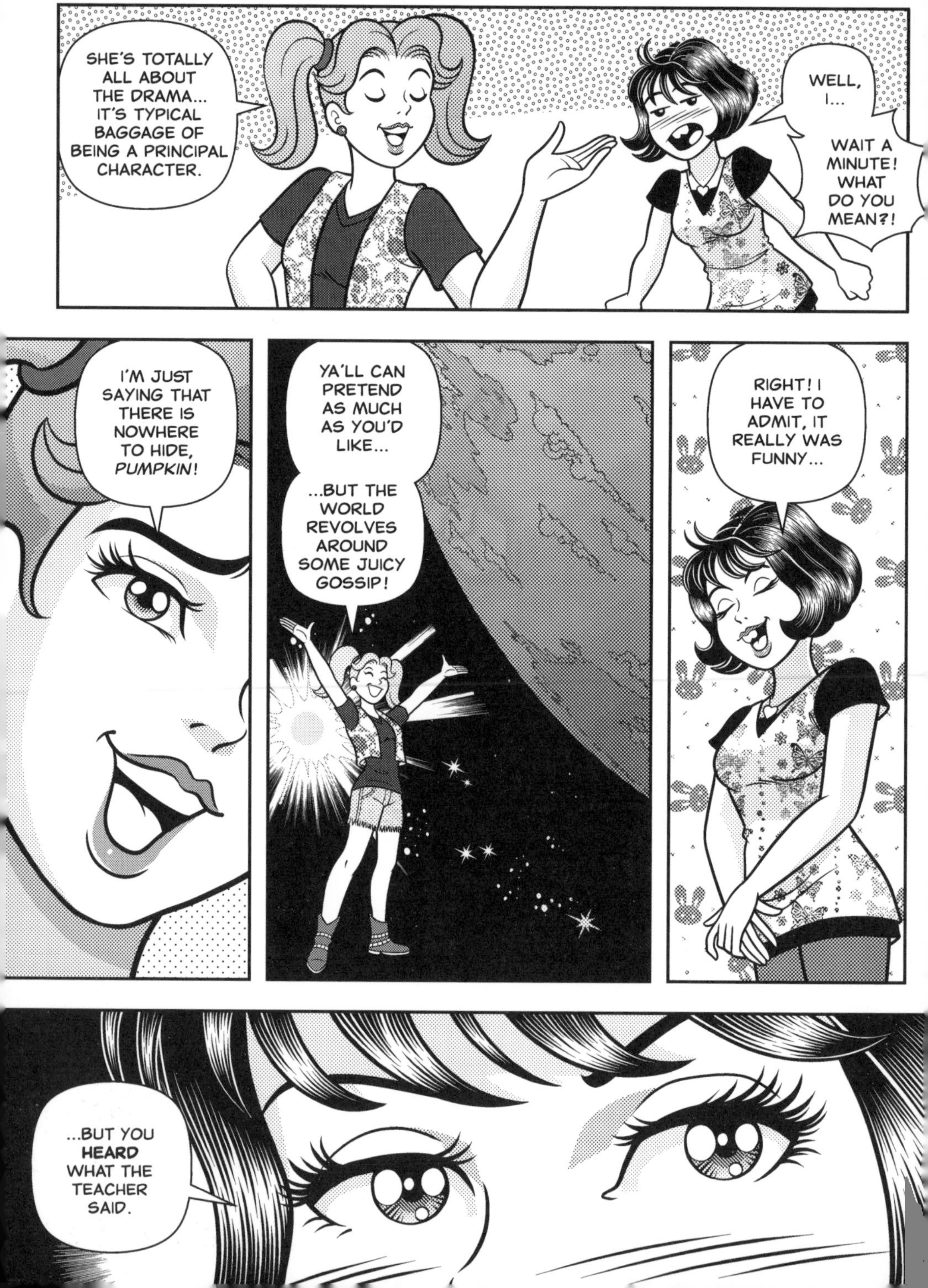
SHE'S TOTALLY ALL ABOUT THE DRAMA... IT'S TYPICAL BAGGAGE OF BEING A PRINCIPAL CHARACTER.
WELL, I...
WAIT A MINUTE! WHAT DO YOU MEAN?!
I'M JUST SAYING THAT THERE IS NOWHERE TO HIDE, *PUMPKIN*!
YA'LL CAN PRETEND AS MUCH AS YOU'D LIKE...
...BUT THE WORLD REVOLVES AROUND SOME JUICY GOSSIP!
RIGHT! I HAVE TO ADMIT, IT REALLY WAS FUNNY...
...BUT YOU **HEARD** WHAT THE TEACHER SAID.

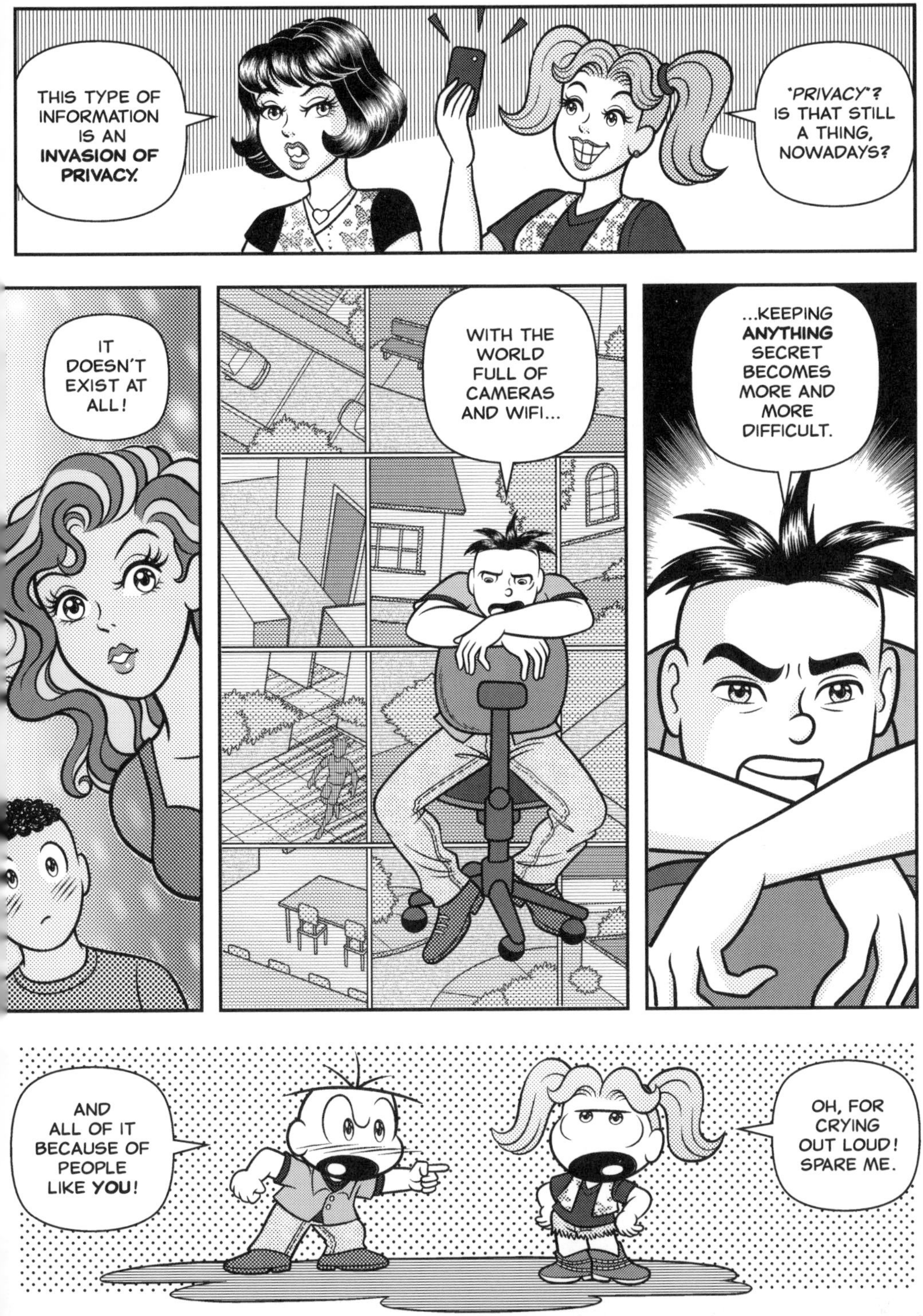
THIS TYPE OF INFORMATION IS AN **INVASION OF PRIVACY.**
"*PRIVACY*"? IS THAT STILL A THING, NOWADAYS?
IT DOESN'T EXIST AT ALL!
WITH THE WORLD FULL OF CAMERAS AND WIFI...
...KEEPING **ANYTHING** SECRET BECOMES MORE AND MORE DIFFICULT.
AND ALL OF IT BECAUSE OF PEOPLE LIKE **YOU**!
OH, FOR CRYING OUT LOUD! SPARE ME.

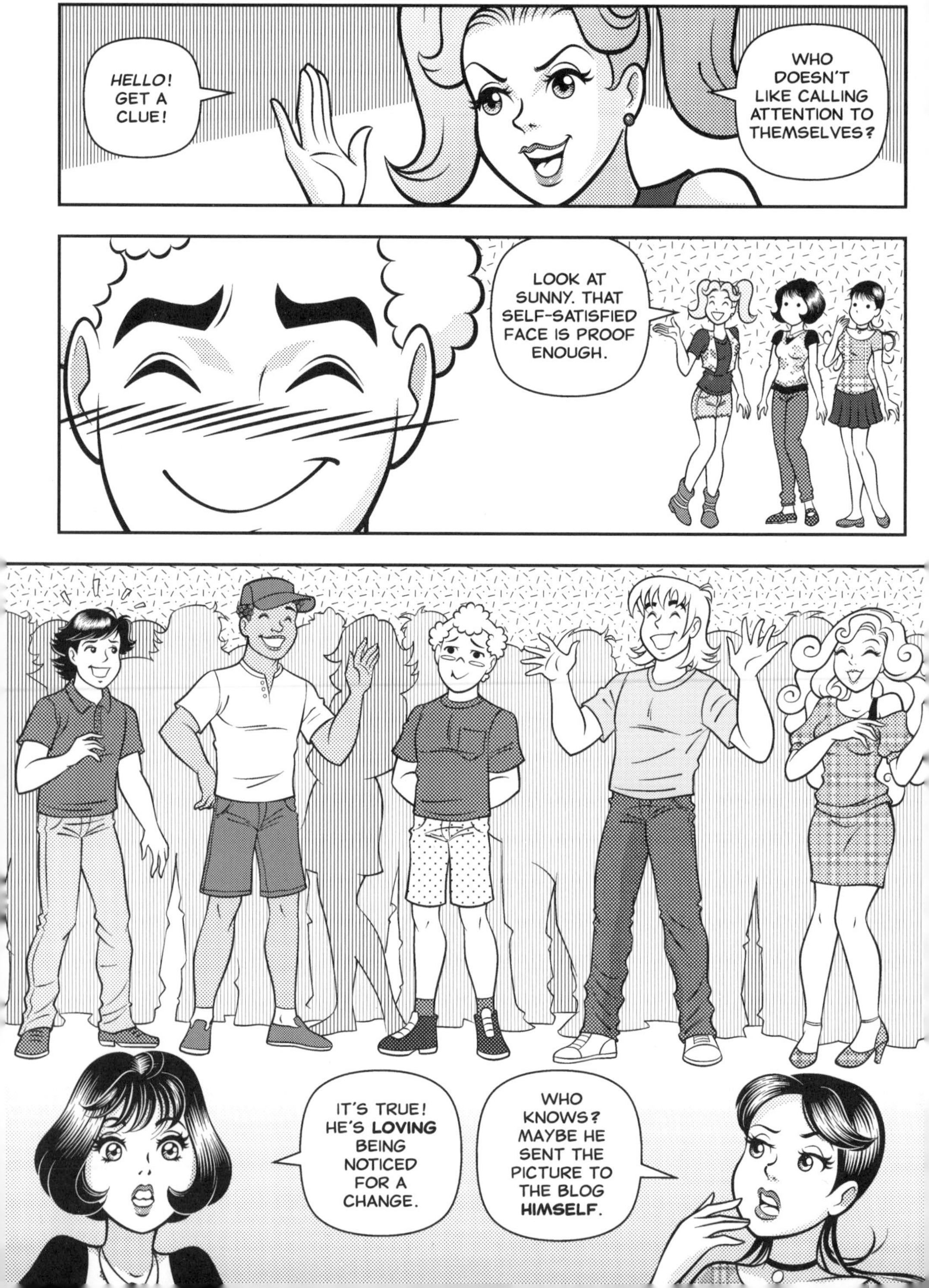
HELLO! GET A CLUE!
WHO DOESN'T LIKE CALLING ATTENTION TO THEMSELVES?
LOOK AT SUNNY. THAT SELF-SATISFIED FACE IS PROOF ENOUGH.
IT'S TRUE! HE'S **LOVING** BEING NOTICED FOR A CHANGE.
WHO KNOWS? MAYBE HE SENT THE PICTURE TO THE BLOG **HIMSELF**.

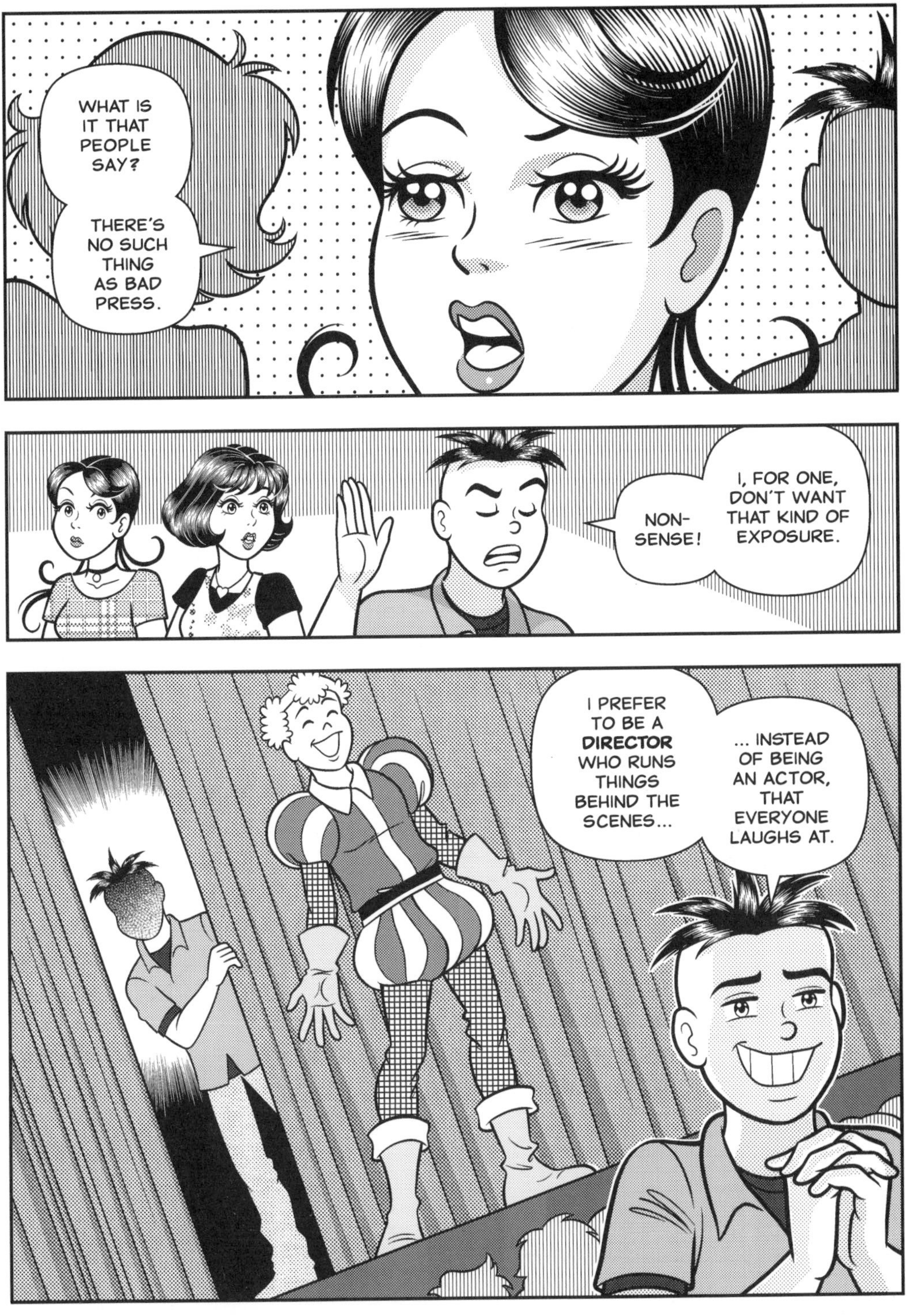
WHAT IS IT THAT PEOPLE SAY?
THERE'S NO SUCH THING AS BAD PRESS.
NON-SENSE!
I, FOR ONE, DON'T WANT THAT KIND OF EXPOSURE.
I PREFER TO BE A **DIRECTOR** WHO RUNS THINGS BEHIND THE SCENES...
... INSTEAD OF BEING AN ACTOR, THAT EVERYONE LAUGHS AT.

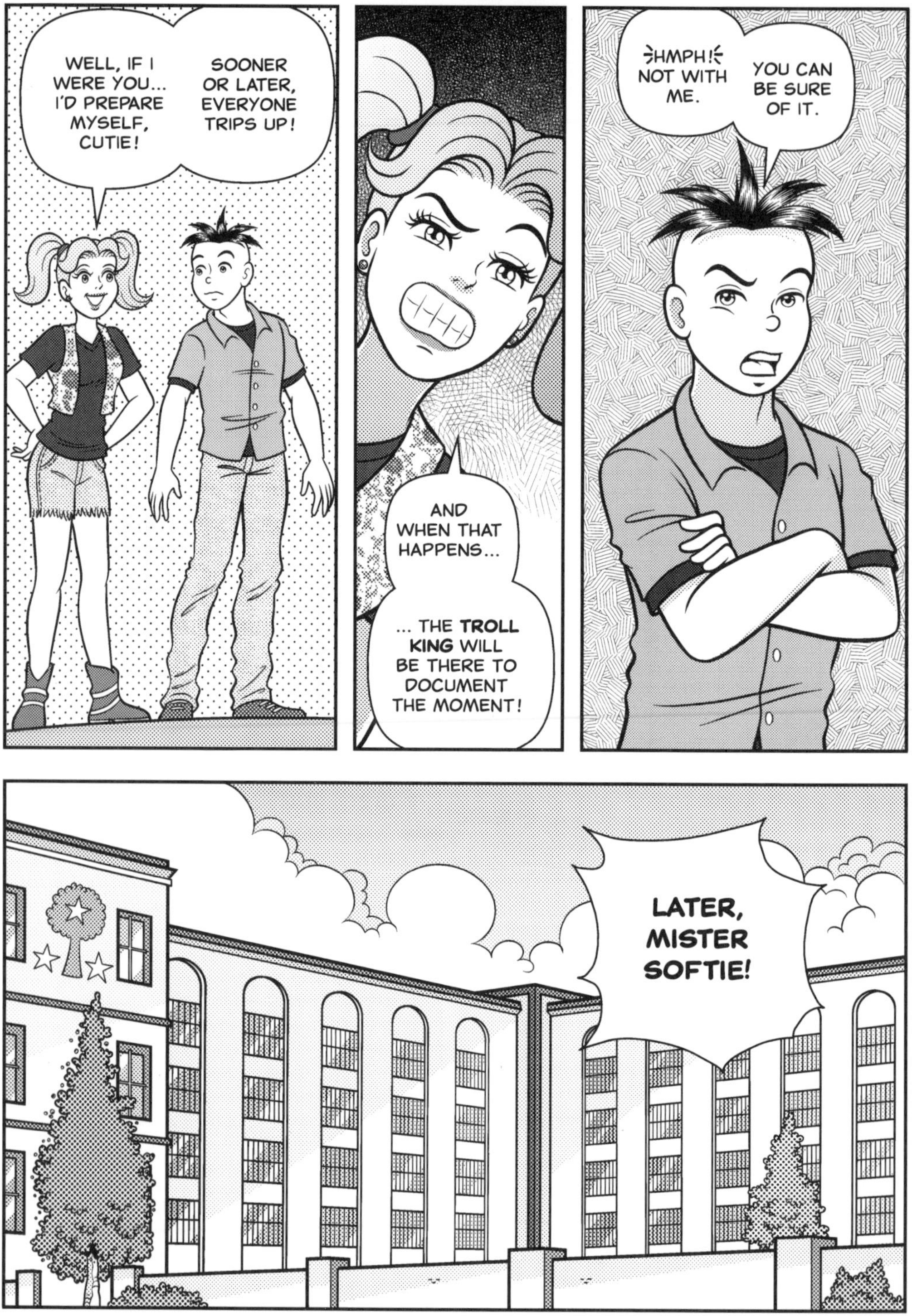
WELL, IF I WERE YOU... I'D PREPARE MYSELF, CUTIE!
SOONER OR LATER, EVERYONE TRIPS UP!
AND WHEN THAT HAPPENS...
... THE **TROLL KING** WILL BE THERE TO DOCUMENT THE MOMENT!
HMPH! NOT WITH ME.
YOU CAN BE SURE OF IT.
LATER, MISTER SOFTIE!

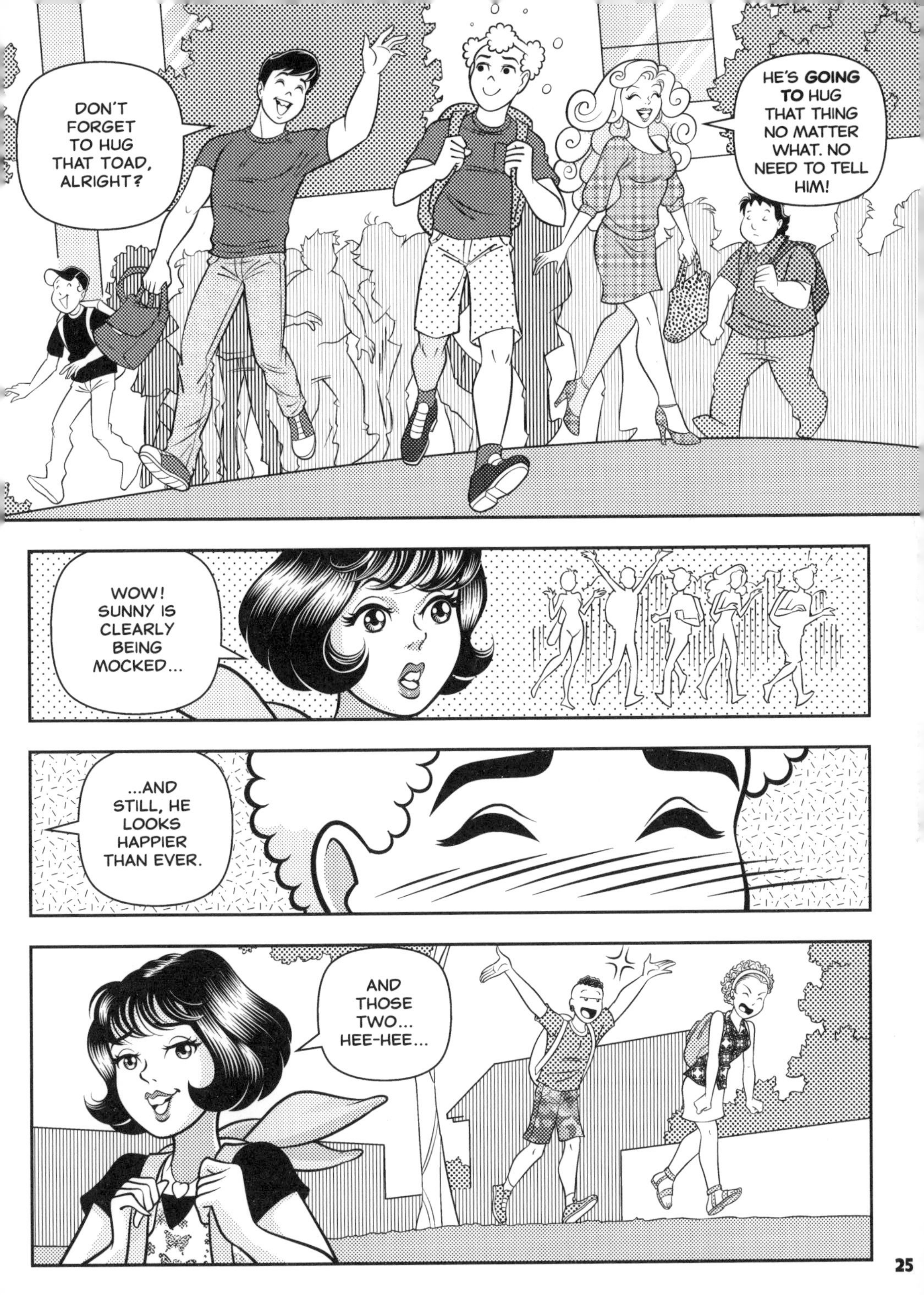
DON'T FORGET TO HUG THAT TOAD, ALRIGHT?
HE'S **GOING TO** HUG THAT THING NO MATTER WHAT. NO NEED TO TELL HIM!
WOW! SUNNY IS CLEARLY BEING MOCKED...
...AND STILL, HE LOOKS HAPPIER THAN EVER.
AND THOSE TWO... HEE-HEE...

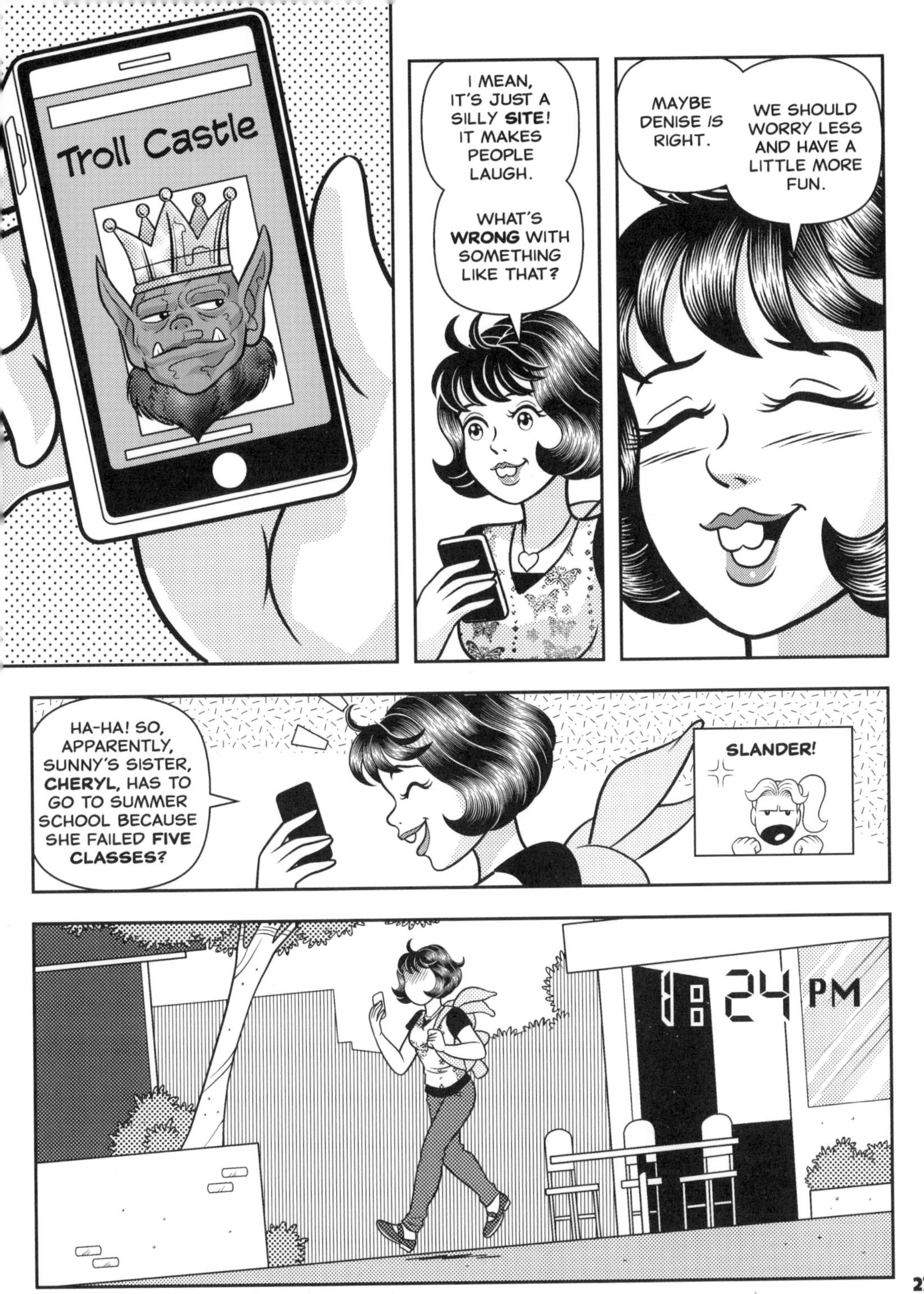
Troll Castle
I MEAN, IT'S JUST A SILLY **SITE**! IT MAKES PEOPLE LAUGH.
WHAT'S **WRONG** WITH SOMETHING LIKE THAT?
MAYBE DENISE IS RIGHT.
WE SHOULD WORRY LESS AND HAVE A LITTLE MORE FUN.
HA-HA! SO, APPARENTLY, SUNNY'S SISTER, **CHERYL**, HAS TO GO TO SUMMER SCHOOL BECAUSE SHE FAILED **FIVE CLASSES**?
SLANDER!
24 PM

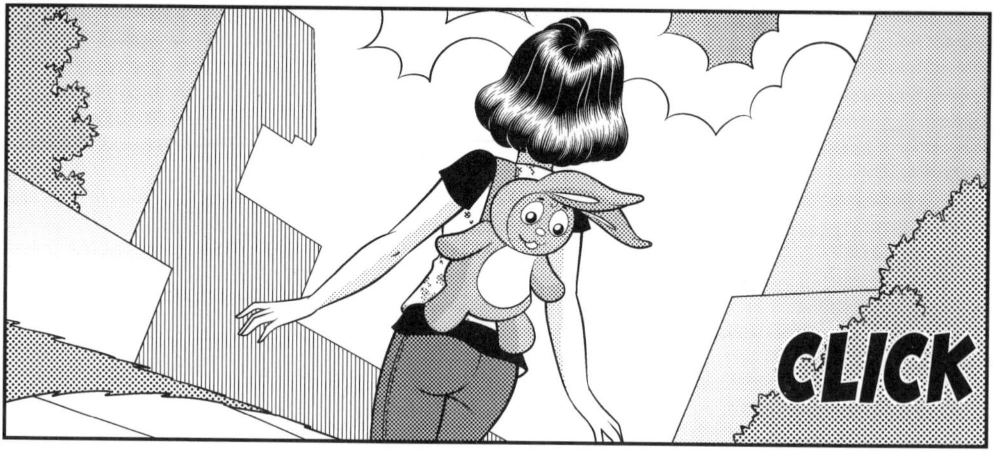
CLICK
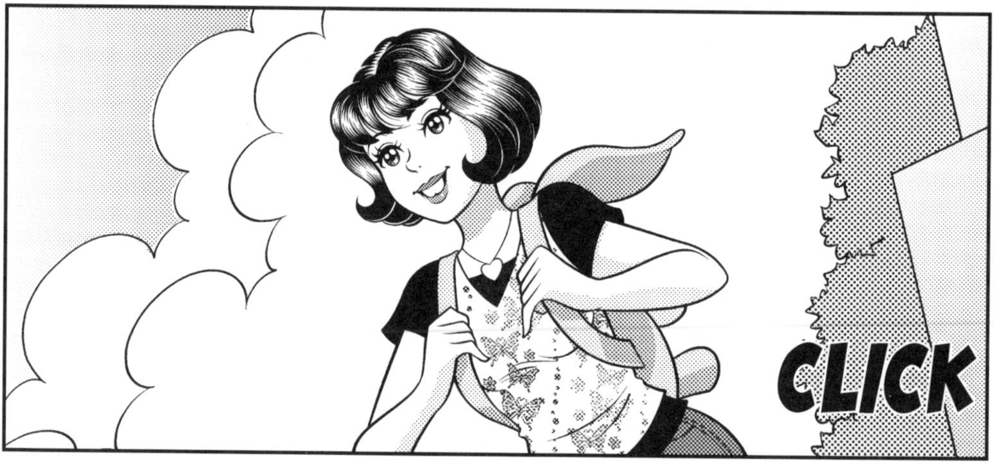
CLICK
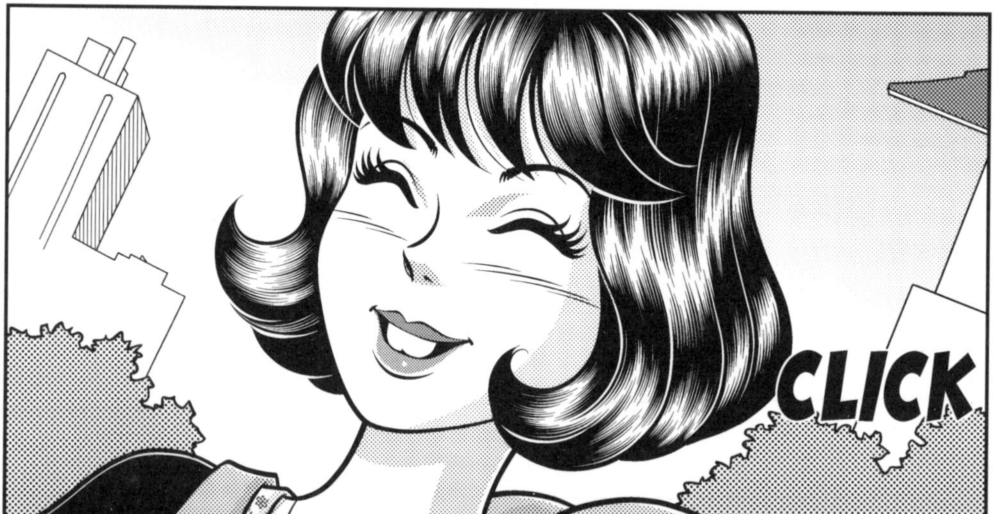
CLICK

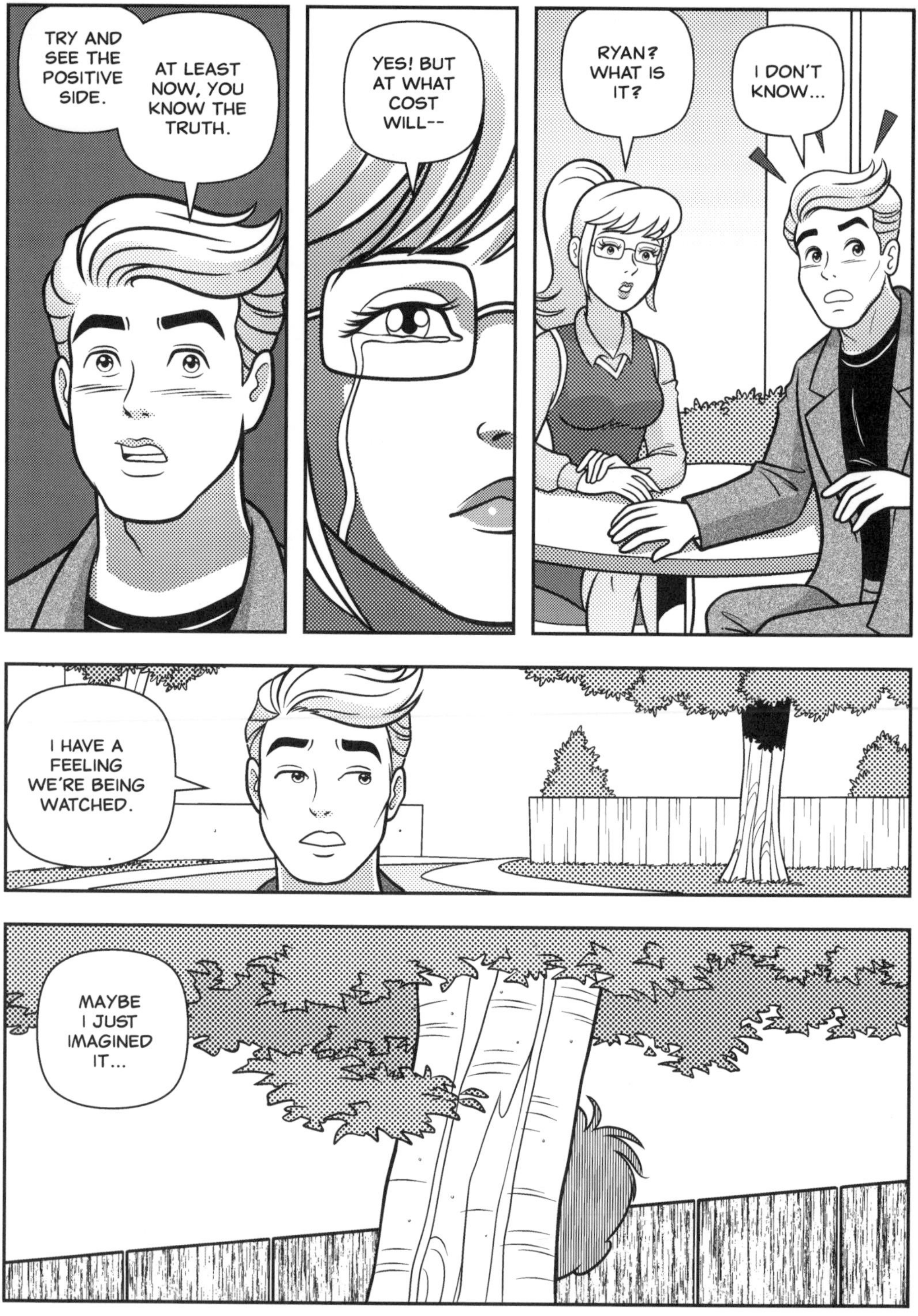
TRY AND SEE THE POSITIVE SIDE.
AT LEAST NOW, YOU KNOW THE TRUTH.
YES! BUT AT WHAT COST WILL--
RYAN? WHAT IS IT?
I DON'T KNOW...
I HAVE A FEELING WE'RE BEING WATCHED.
MAYBE I JUST IMAGINED IT...

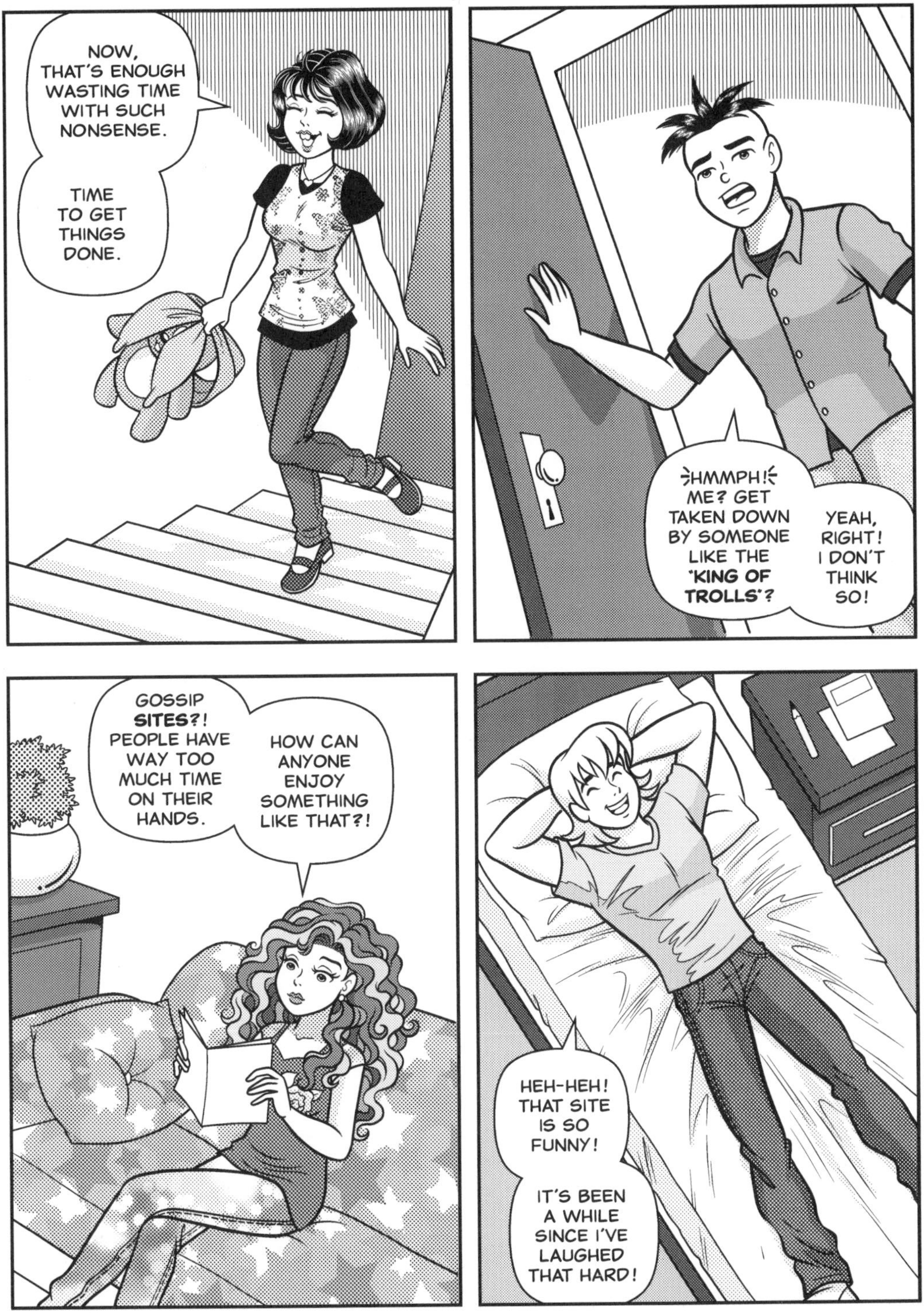
NOW, THAT'S ENOUGH WASTING TIME WITH SUCH NONSENSE.
TIME TO GET THINGS DONE.
HMMPH! ME? GET TAKEN DOWN BY SOMEONE LIKE THE "KING OF TROLLS"?
YEAH, RIGHT! I DON'T THINK SO!
GOSSIP SITES?! PEOPLE HAVE WAY TOO MUCH TIME ON THEIR HANDS.
HOW CAN ANYONE ENJOY SOMETHING LIKE THAT?!
HEH-HEH! THAT SITE IS SO FUNNY!
IT'S BEEN A WHILE SINCE I'VE LAUGHED THAT HARD!

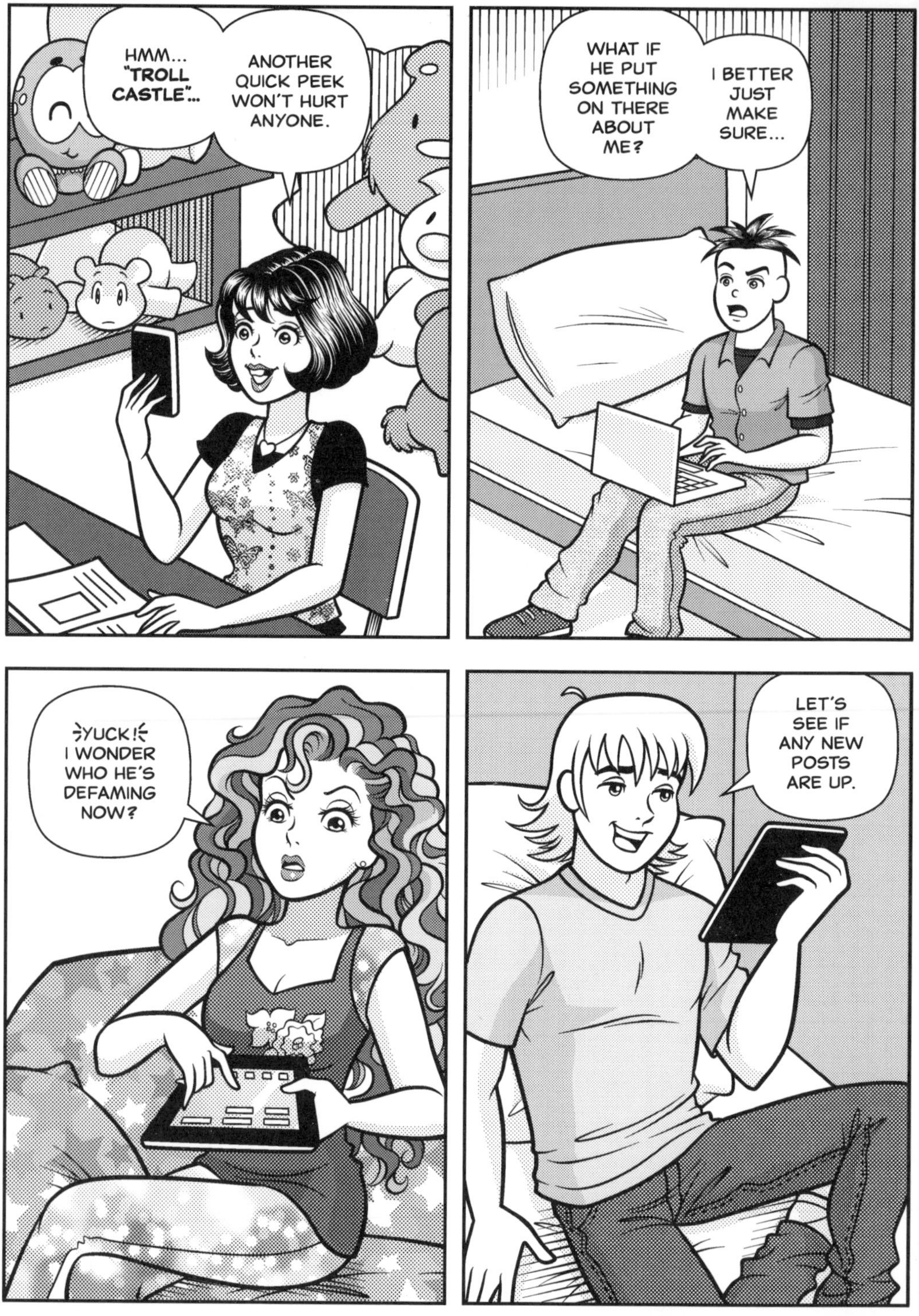
HMM... "TROLL CASTLE"...
ANOTHER QUICK PEEK WON'T HURT ANYONE.
WHAT IF HE PUT SOMETHING ON THERE ABOUT ME?
I BETTER JUST MAKE SURE...
YUCK! I WONDER WHO HE'S DEFAMING NOW?
LET'S SEE IF ANY NEW POSTS ARE UP.

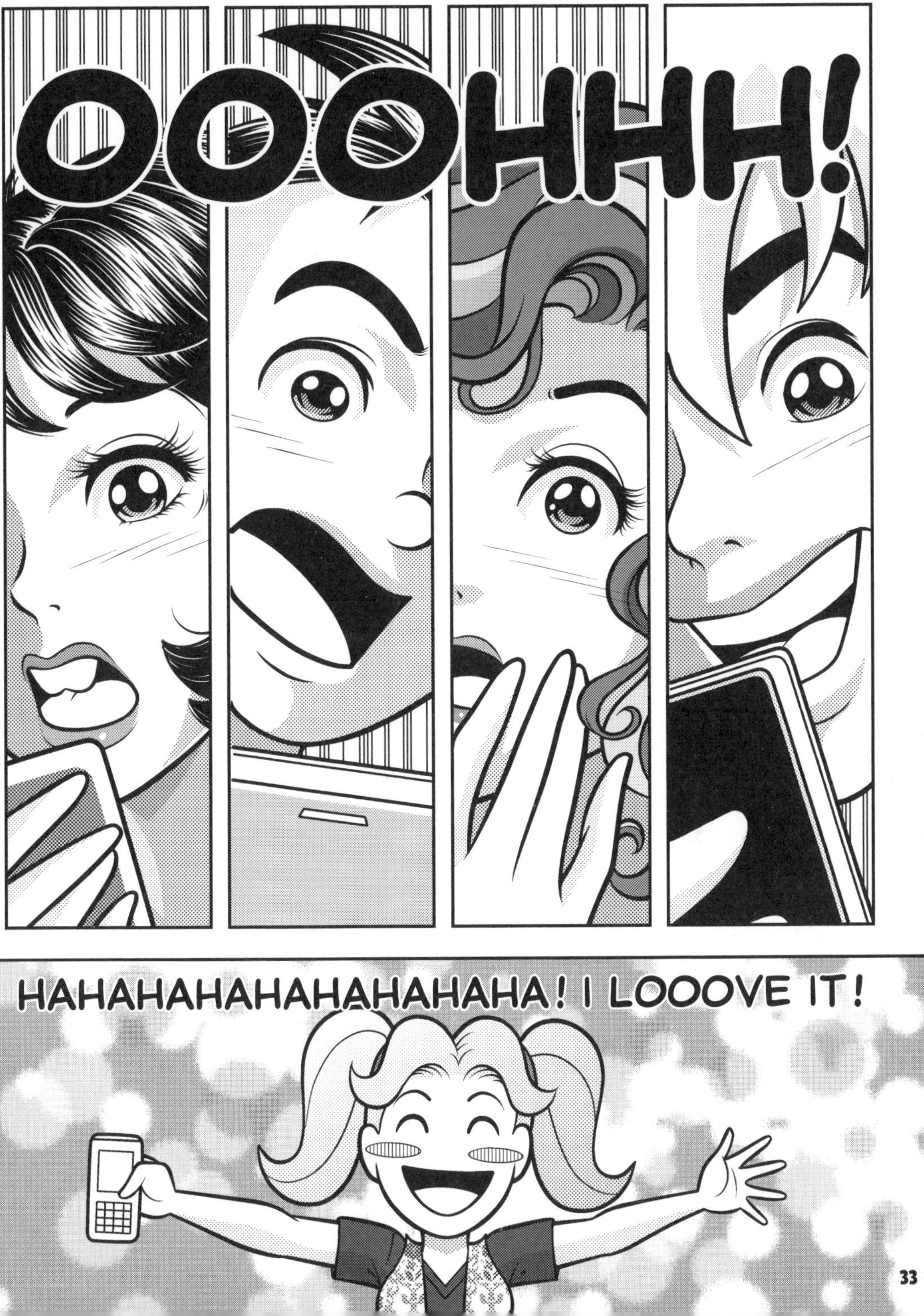
OOOHHH!
HAHAHAHAHAHAHAHAHA! I LOOOVE IT!

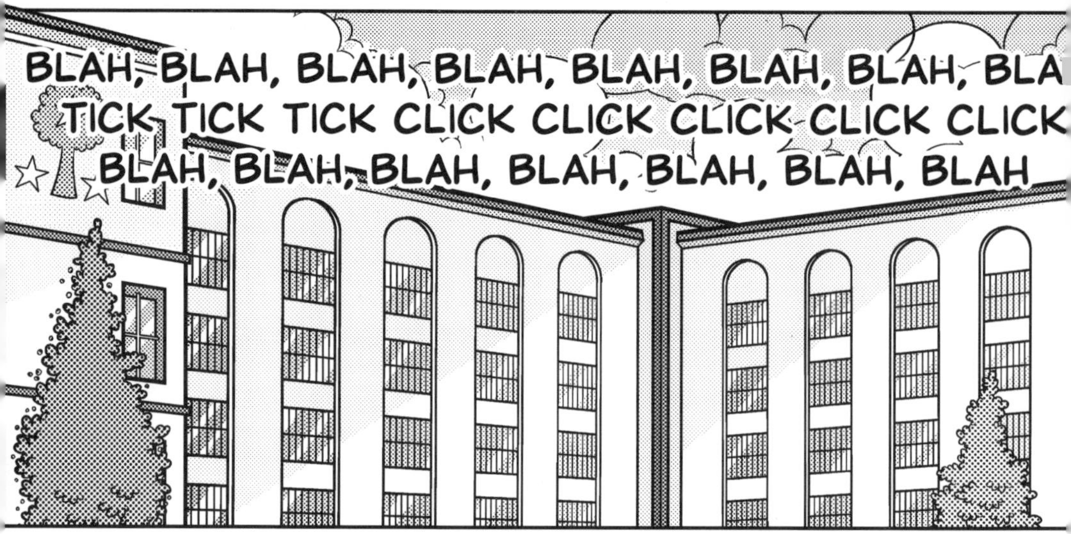
BLAH, BLAH, BLAH, BLAH, BLAH, BLAH, BLAH, BLA
TICK TICK TICK CLICK CLICK CLICK CLICK CLICK
BLAH, BLAH, BLAH, BLAH, BLAH, BLAH, BLAH

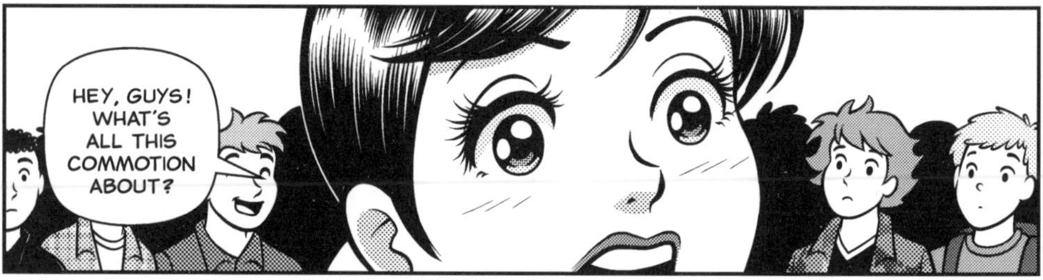
HEY, GUYS! WHAT'S ALL THIS COMMOTION ABOUT?

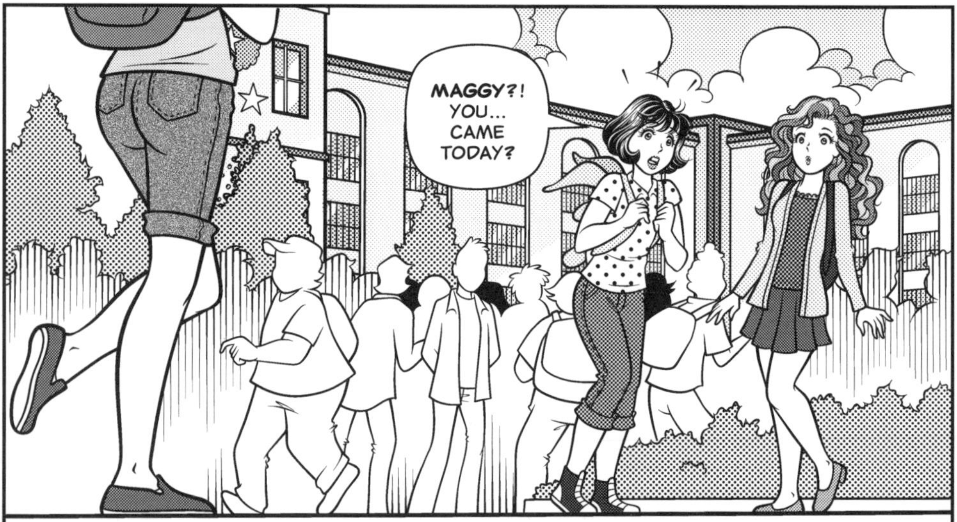
MAGGY?! YOU... CAME TODAY?

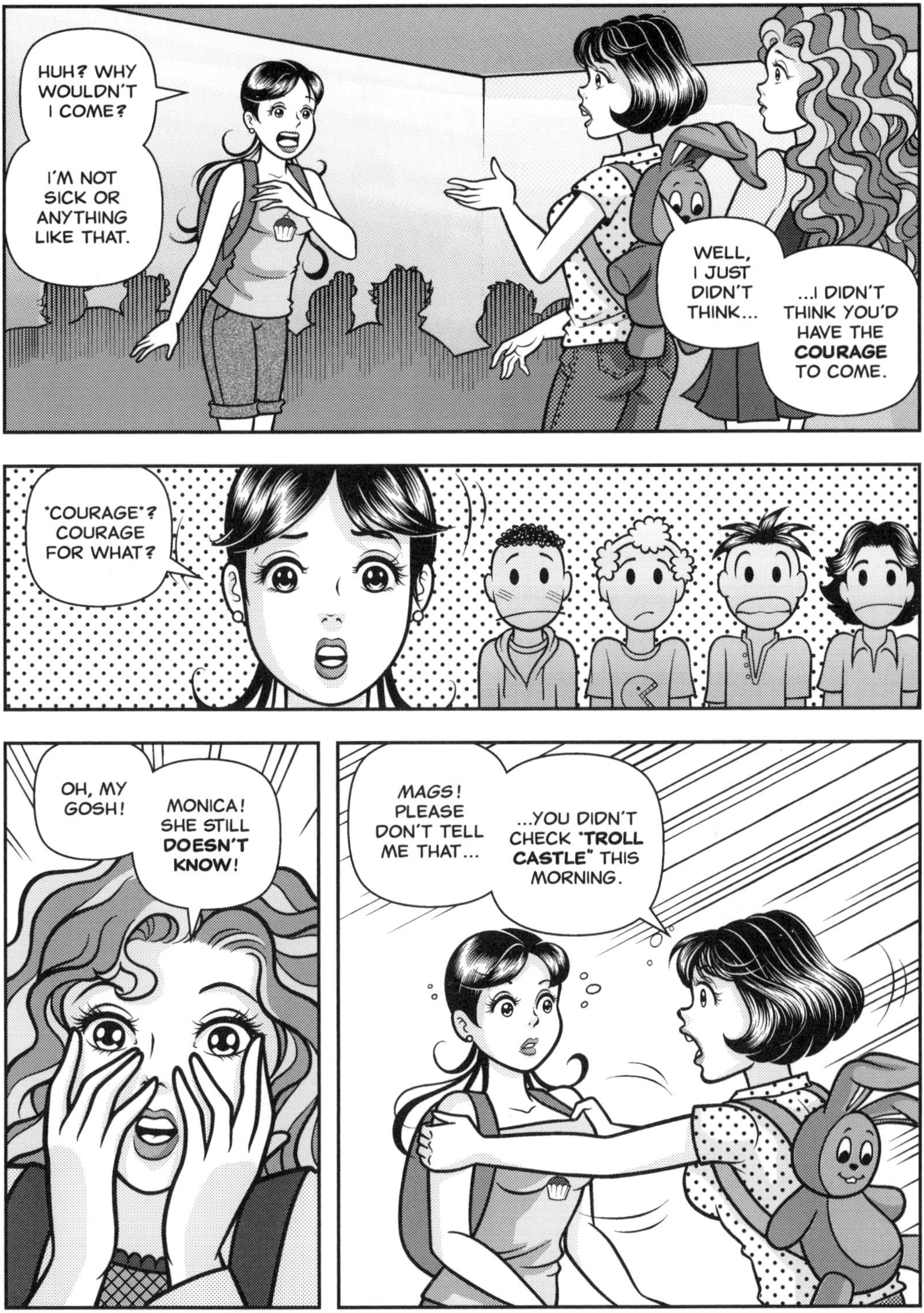
HUH? WHY WOULDN'T I COME?
I'M NOT SICK OR ANYTHING LIKE THAT.
WELL, I JUST DIDN'T THINK...
...I DIDN'T THINK YOU'D HAVE THE **COURAGE** TO COME.
"COURAGE"? COURAGE FOR WHAT?
OH, MY GOSH!
MONICA! SHE STILL **DOESN'T KNOW**!
MAGS! PLEASE DON'T TELL ME THAT...
...YOU DIDN'T CHECK **"TROLL CASTLE"** THIS MORNING.

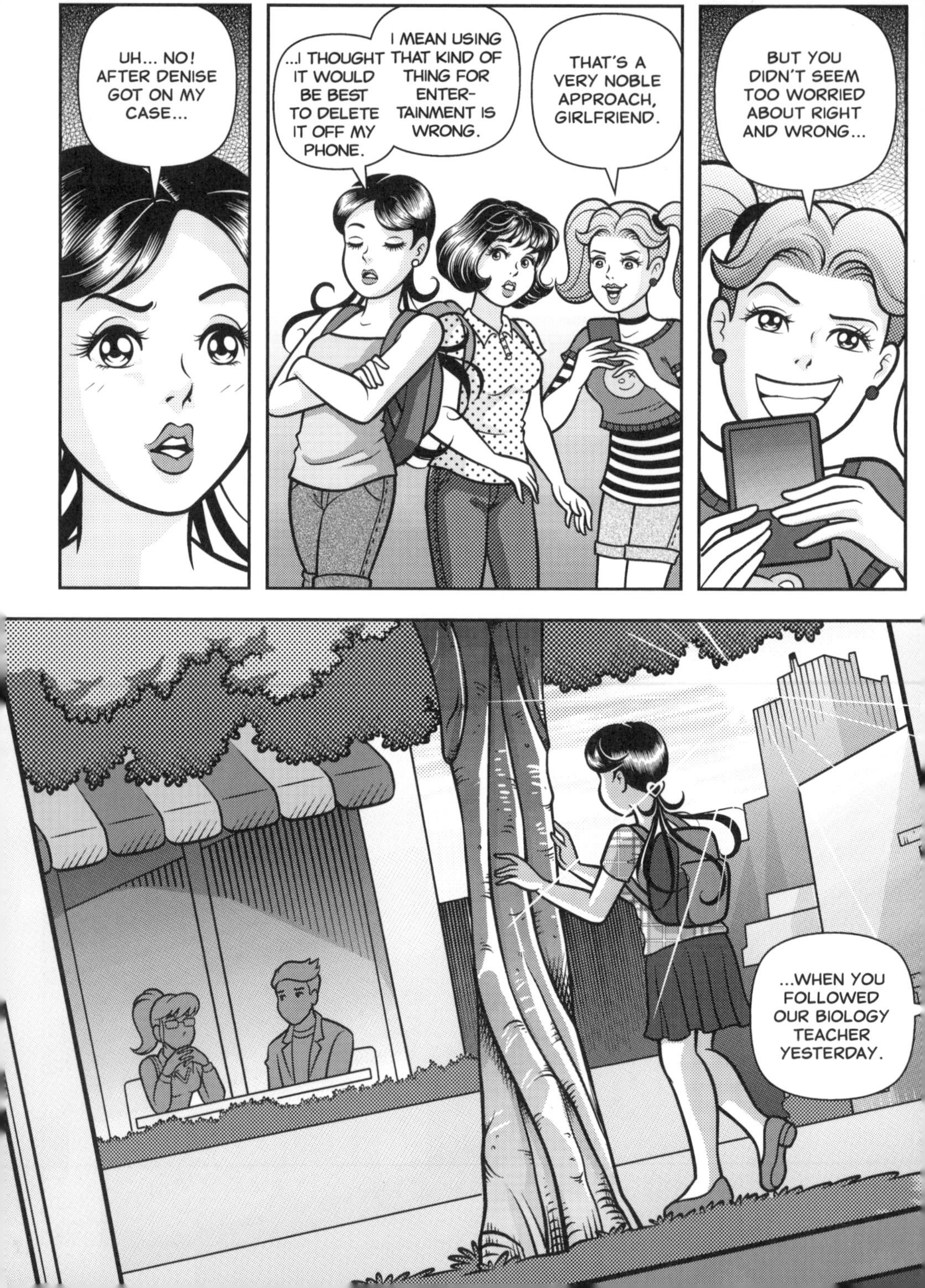
UH... NO! AFTER DENISE GOT ON MY CASE...
...I THOUGHT IT WOULD BE BEST TO DELETE IT OFF MY PHONE.
I MEAN USING THAT KIND OF THING FOR ENTER-TAINMENT IS WRONG.
THAT'S A VERY NOBLE APPROACH, GIRLFRIEND.
BUT YOU DIDN'T SEEM TOO WORRIED ABOUT RIGHT AND WRONG...
...WHEN YOU FOLLOWED OUR BIOLOGY TEACHER YESTERDAY.

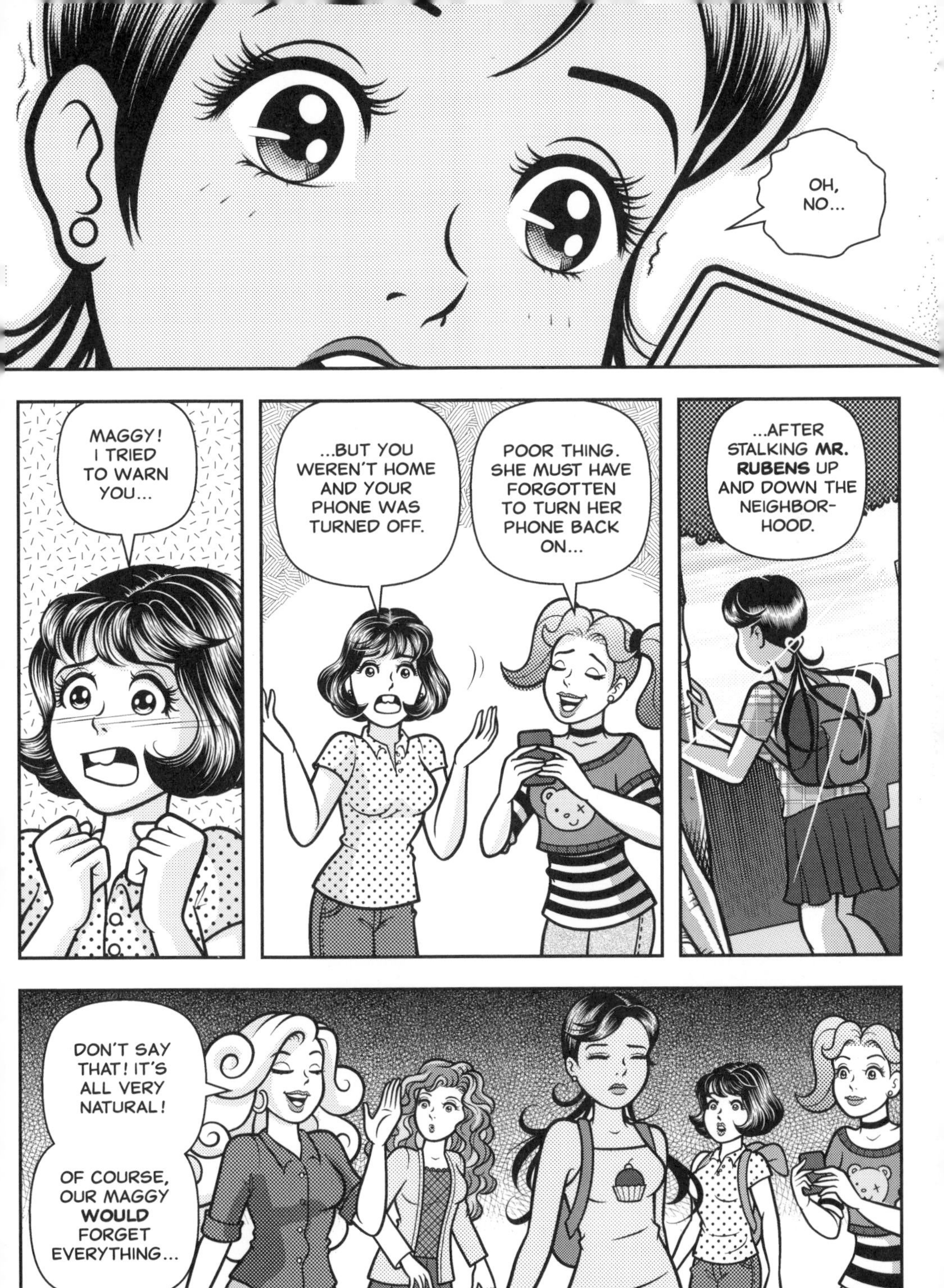
OH, NO...
MAGGY! I TRIED TO WARN YOU...
...BUT YOU WEREN'T HOME AND YOUR PHONE WAS TURNED OFF.
POOR THING. SHE MUST HAVE FORGOTTEN TO TURN HER PHONE BACK ON...
...AFTER STALKING **MR. RUBENS** UP AND DOWN THE NEIGHBOR-HOOD.
DON'T SAY THAT! IT'S ALL VERY NATURAL!
OF COURSE, OUR MAGGY **WOULD** FORGET EVERYTHING...

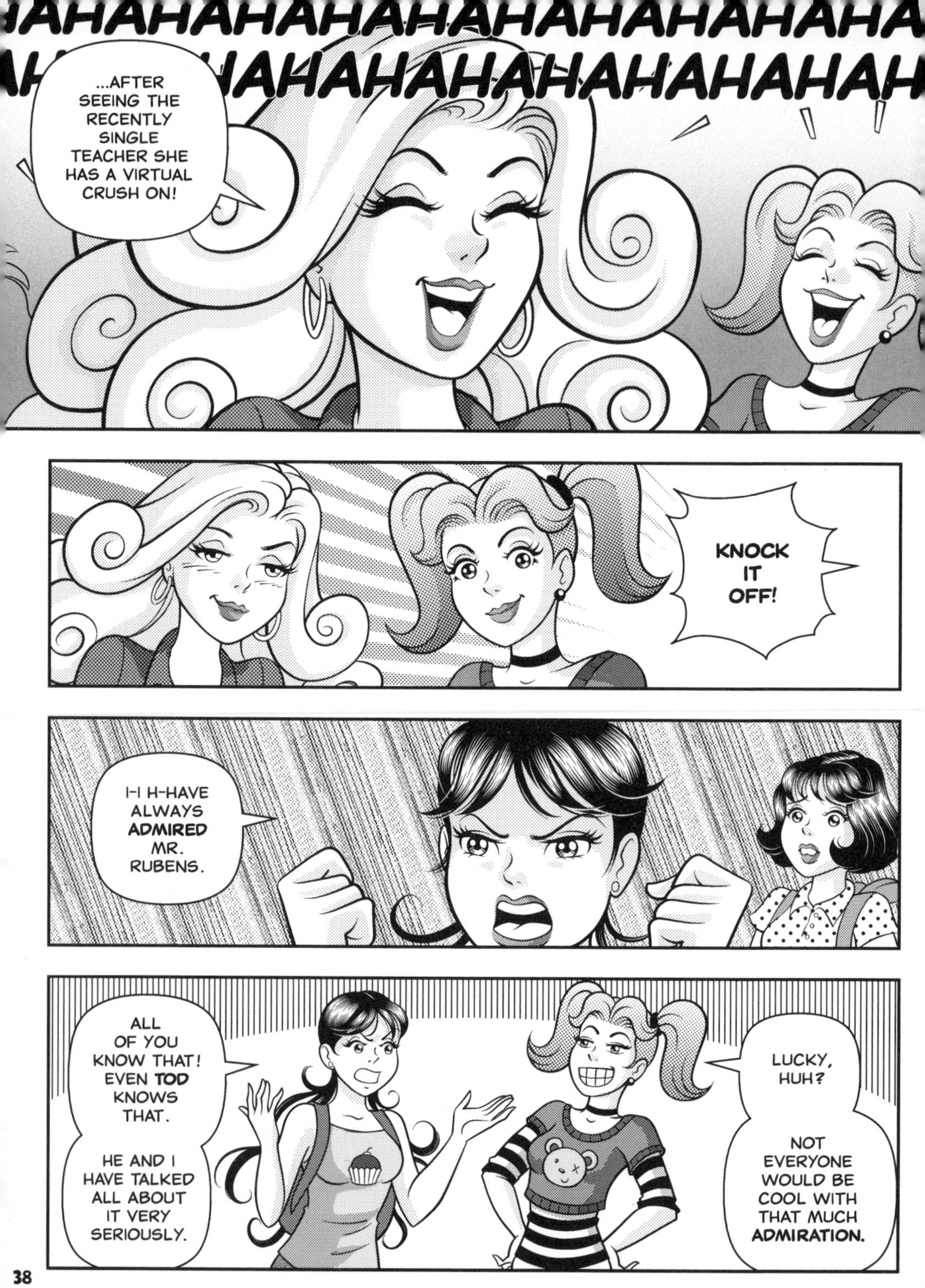
AHAHAHAHAHAHAHAHAHAHAHAHA
AHAHAHAHAHAHAHAHAHAHAHAH
...AFTER SEEING THE RECENTLY SINGLE TEACHER SHE HAS A VIRTUAL CRUSH ON!
KNOCK IT OFF!
I-I H-HAVE ALWAYS **ADMIRED** MR. RUBENS.
ALL OF YOU KNOW THAT! EVEN **TOD** KNOWS THAT.
HE AND I HAVE TALKED ALL ABOUT IT VERY SERIOUSLY.
LUCKY, HUH?
NOT EVERYONE WOULD BE COOL WITH THAT MUCH **ADMIRATION.**

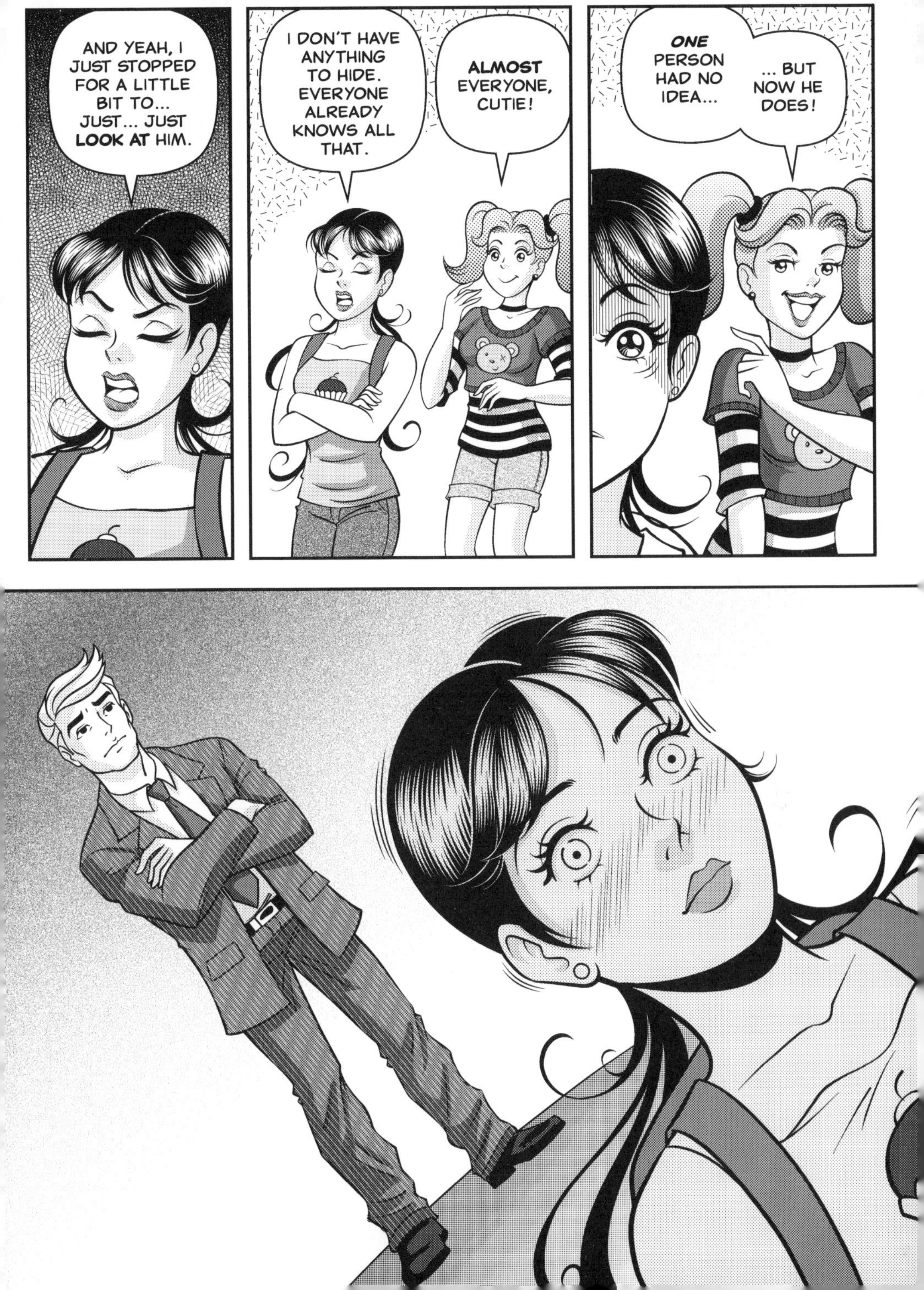
AND YEAH, I JUST STOPPED FOR A LITTLE BIT TO... JUST... JUST **LOOK AT** HIM.
I DON'T HAVE ANYTHING TO HIDE. EVERYONE ALREADY KNOWS ALL THAT.
ALMOST EVERYONE, CUTIE!
ONE PERSON HAD NO IDEA...
... BUT NOW HE DOES!

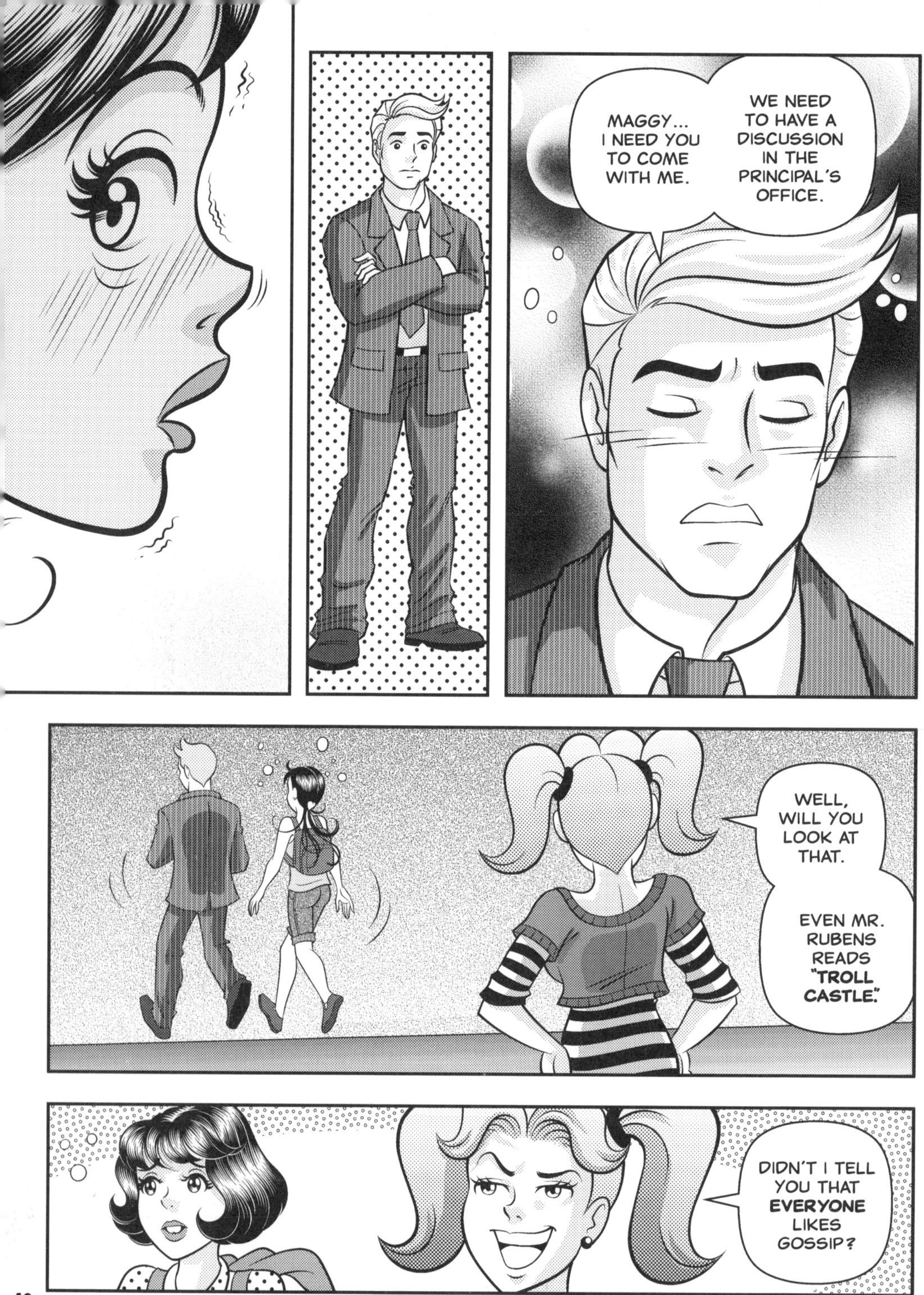

MAGGY... I NEED YOU TO COME WITH ME.
WE NEED TO HAVE A DISCUSSION IN THE PRINCIPAL'S OFFICE.
WELL, WILL YOU LOOK AT THAT.
EVEN MR. RUBENS READS "TROLL CASTLE."
DIDN'T I TELL YOU THAT EVERYONE LIKES GOSSIP?

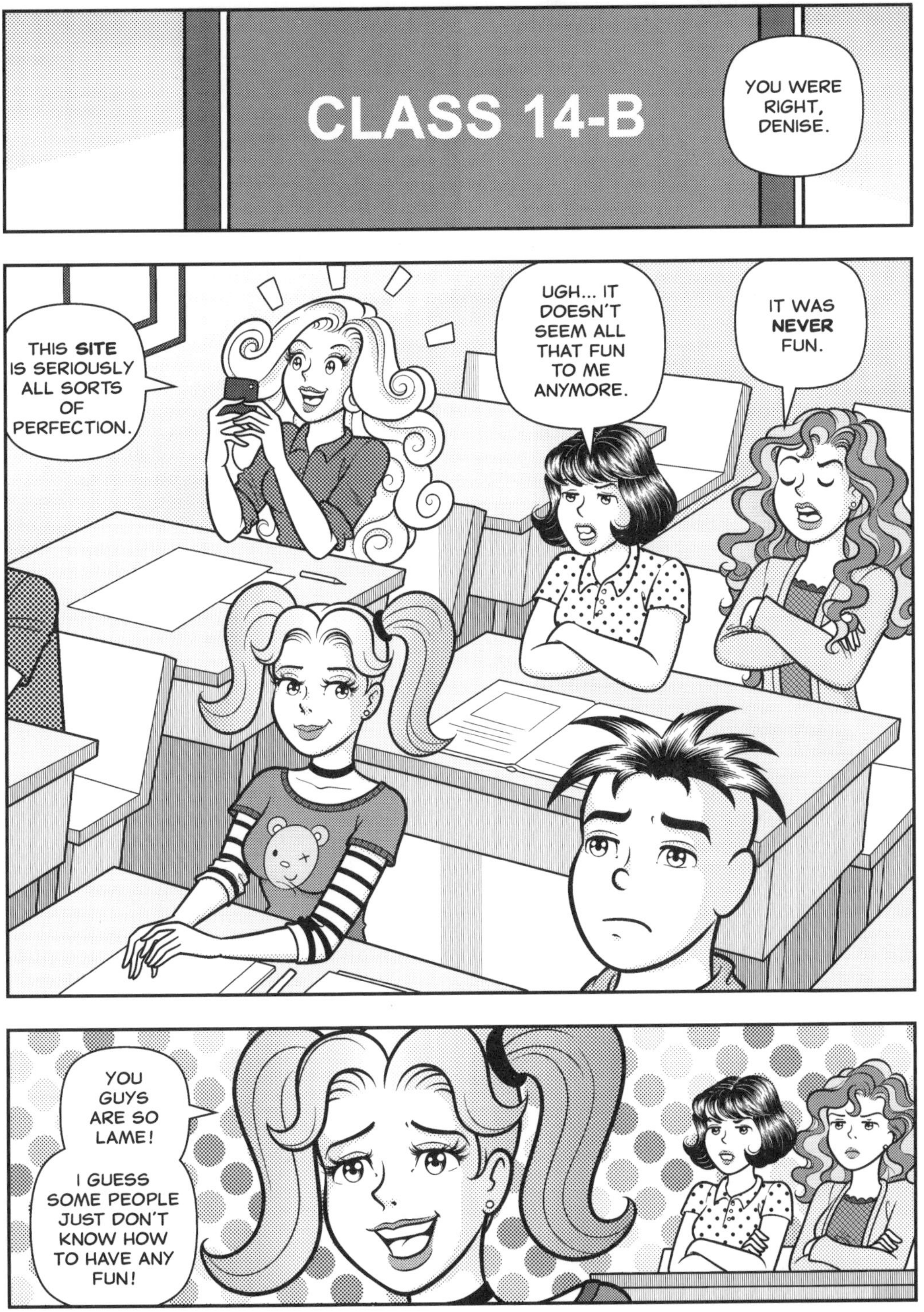
CLASS 14-B
YOU WERE RIGHT, DENISE.
THIS SITE IS SERIOUSLY ALL SORTS OF PERFECTION.
UGH... IT DOESN'T SEEM ALL THAT FUN TO ME ANYMORE.
IT WAS NEVER FUN.
YOU GUYS ARE SO LAME!
I GUESS SOME PEOPLE JUST DON'T KNOW HOW TO HAVE ANY FUN!

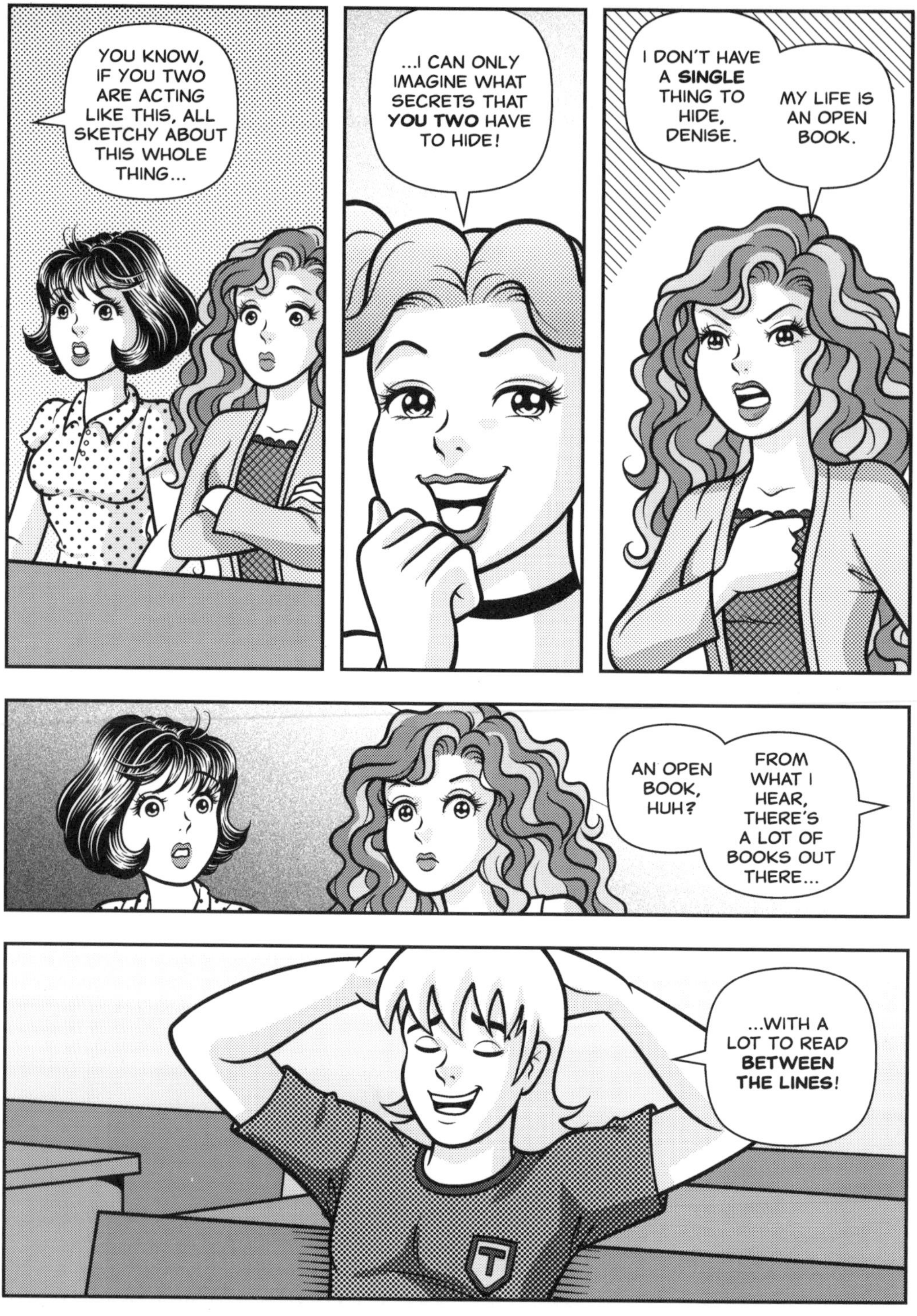
YOU KNOW, IF YOU TWO ARE ACTING LIKE THIS, ALL SKETCHY ABOUT THIS WHOLE THING...
...I CAN ONLY IMAGINE WHAT SECRETS THAT **YOU TWO** HAVE TO HIDE!
I DON'T HAVE A **SINGLE** THING TO HIDE, DENISE.
MY LIFE IS AN OPEN BOOK.
AN OPEN BOOK, HUH?
FROM WHAT I HEAR, THERE'S A LOT OF BOOKS OUT THERE...
...WITH A LOT TO READ **BETWEEN THE LINES**!

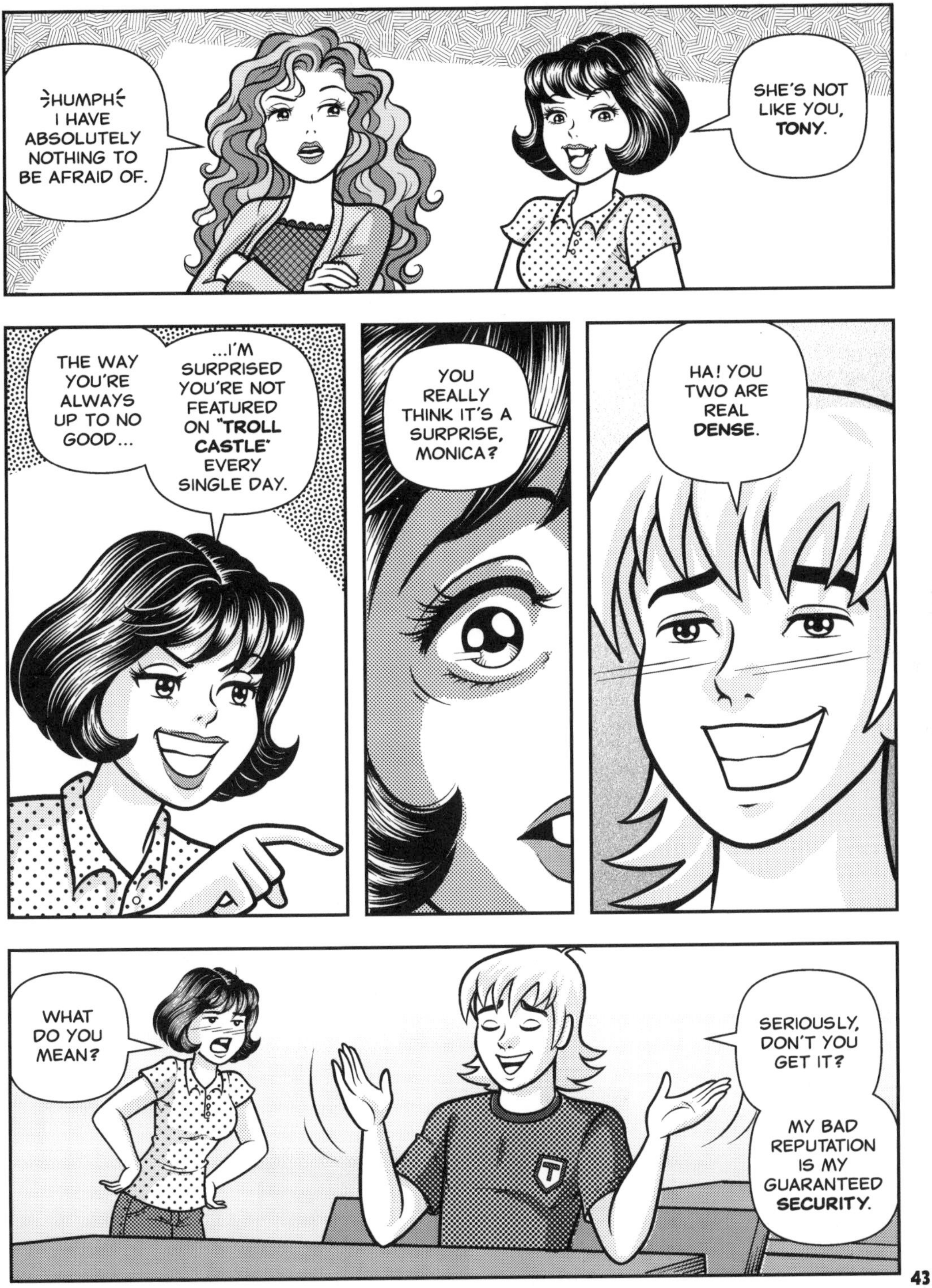

⋟HUMPH⋞ I HAVE ABSOLUTELY NOTHING TO BE AFRAID OF.
SHE'S NOT LIKE YOU, **TONY**.
THE WAY YOU'RE ALWAYS UP TO NO GOOD...
...I'M SURPRISED YOU'RE NOT FEATURED ON "**TROLL CASTLE**" EVERY SINGLE DAY.
YOU REALLY THINK IT'S A SURPRISE, MONICA?
HA! YOU TWO ARE REAL **DENSE**.
WHAT DO YOU MEAN?
SERIOUSLY, DON'T YOU GET IT?
MY BAD REPUTATION IS MY GUARANTEED **SECURITY**.

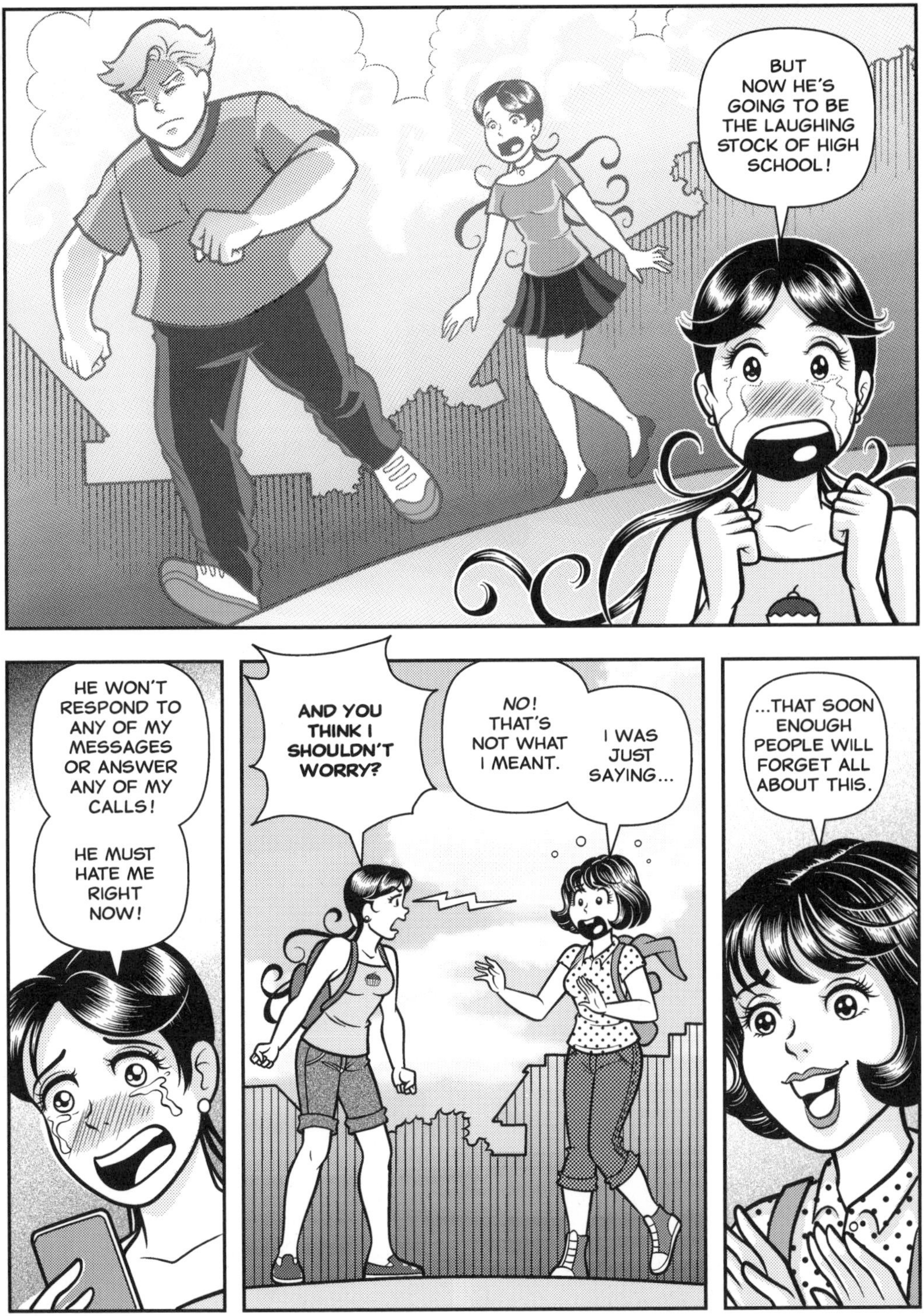
BUT NOW HE'S GOING TO BE THE LAUGHING STOCK OF HIGH SCHOOL!
HE WON'T RESPOND TO ANY OF MY MESSAGES OR ANSWER ANY OF MY CALLS!
HE MUST HATE ME RIGHT NOW!
AND YOU THINK I SHOULDN'T WORRY?
NO! THAT'S NOT WHAT I MEANT.
I WAS JUST SAYING...
...THAT SOON ENOUGH PEOPLE WILL FORGET ALL ABOUT THIS.

49

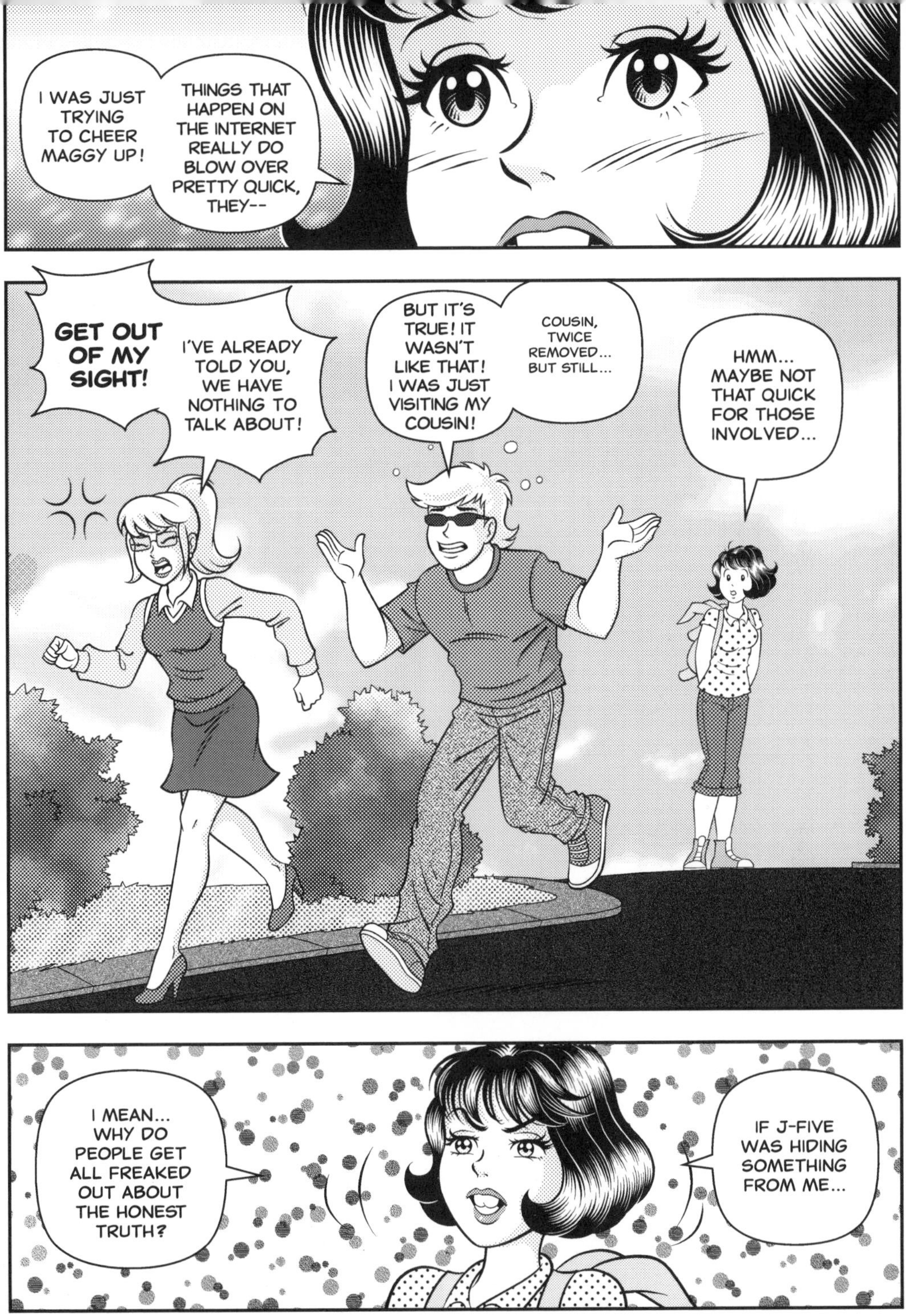

I WAS JUST TRYING TO CHEER MAGGY UP!
THINGS THAT HAPPEN ON THE INTERNET REALLY DO BLOW OVER PRETTY QUICK, THEY--
GET OUT OF MY SIGHT!
I'VE ALREADY TOLD YOU, WE HAVE NOTHING TO TALK ABOUT!
BUT IT'S TRUE! IT WASN'T LIKE THAT! I WAS JUST VISITING MY COUSIN!
COUSIN, TWICE REMOVED... BUT STILL...
HMM... MAYBE NOT THAT QUICK FOR THOSE INVOLVED...
I MEAN... WHY DO PEOPLE GET ALL FREAKED OUT ABOUT THE HONEST TRUTH?
IF J-FIVE WAS HIDING SOMETHING FROM ME...

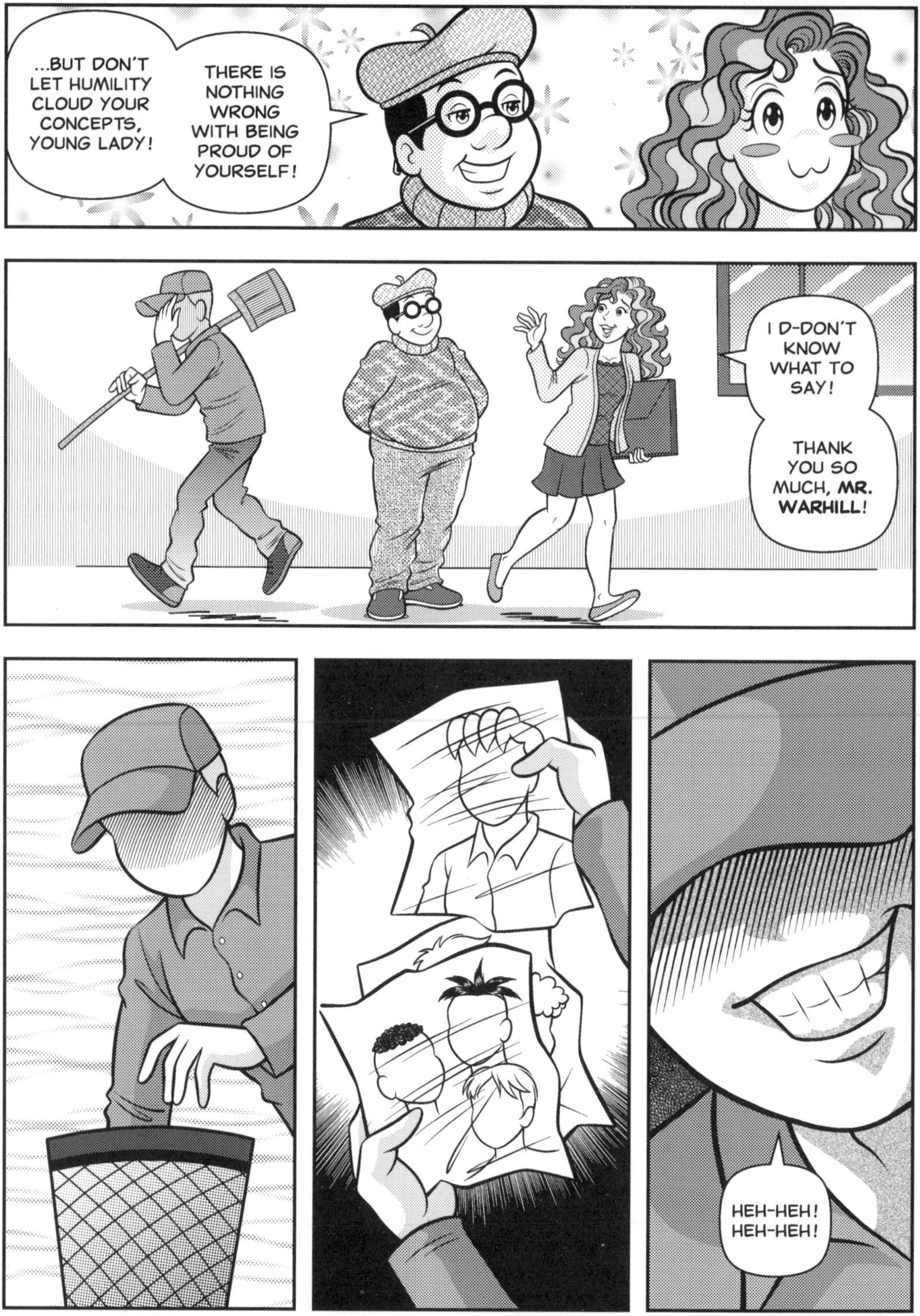
...BUT DON'T LET HUMILITY CLOUD YOUR CONCEPTS, YOUNG LADY!
THERE IS NOTHING WRONG WITH BEING PROUD OF YOURSELF!
I D-DON'T KNOW WHAT TO SAY!
THANK YOU SO MUCH, **MR. WARHILL**!
HEH-HEH! HEH-HEH!

Izzy Double Dips Into her Friend's Grief. Can Maggy Stomach the Shame While Her Friend Steals Her Food?

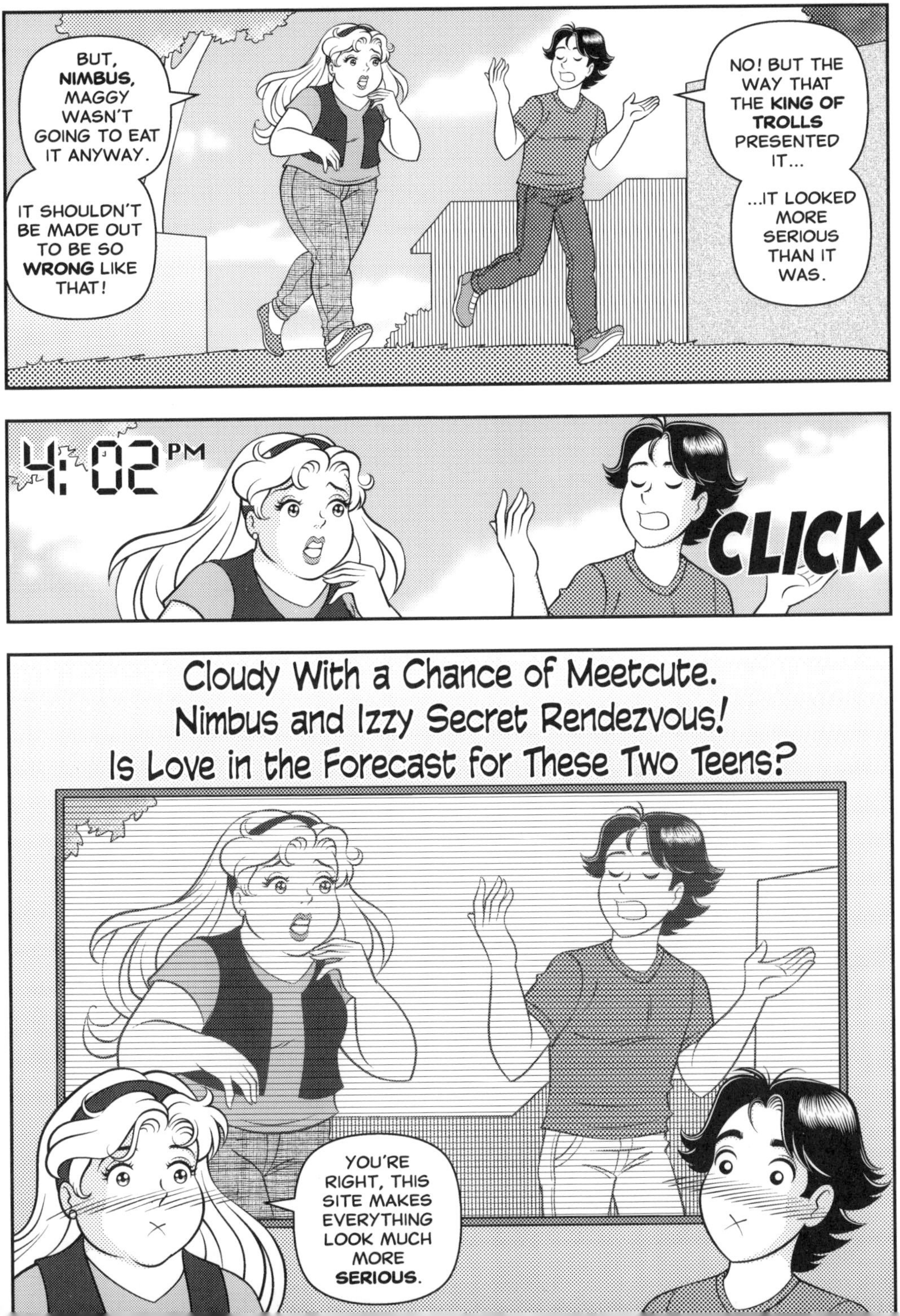
BUT, NIMBUS, MAGGY WASN'T GOING TO EAT IT ANYWAY.
IT SHOULDN'T BE MADE OUT TO BE SO WRONG LIKE THAT!
NO! BUT THE WAY THAT THE KING OF TROLLS PRESENTED IT...
...IT LOOKED MORE SERIOUS THAN IT WAS.
4:02 PM
CLICK
Cloudy With a Chance of Meetcute.
Nimbus and Izzy Secret Rendezvous!
Is Love in the Forecast for These Two Teens?
YOU'RE RIGHT, THIS SITE MAKES EVERYTHING LOOK MUCH MORE SERIOUS.

Insensitive Illusionist Breaks Heart of Ramona the Adolescent Witch

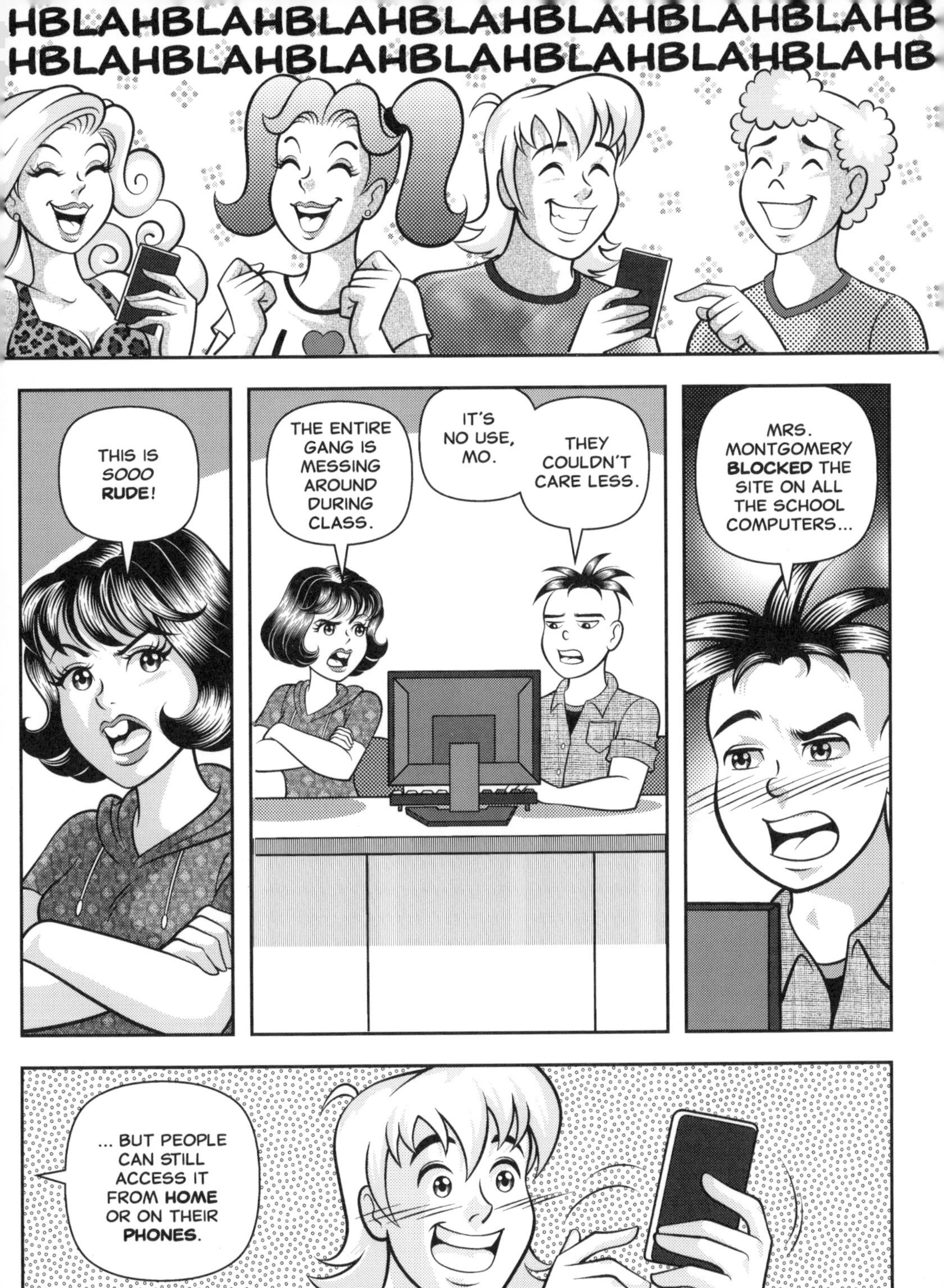
HBLAHBLAHBLAHBLAHBLAHBLAHBLAHB
HBLAHBLAHBLAHBLAHBLAHBLAHBLAHB
THIS IS SOOO RUDE!
THE ENTIRE GANG IS MESSING AROUND DURING CLASS.
IT'S NO USE, MO.
THEY COULDN'T CARE LESS.
MRS. MONTGOMERY BLOCKED THE SITE ON ALL THE SCHOOL COMPUTERS...
... BUT PEOPLE CAN STILL ACCESS IT FROM HOME OR ON THEIR PHONES.

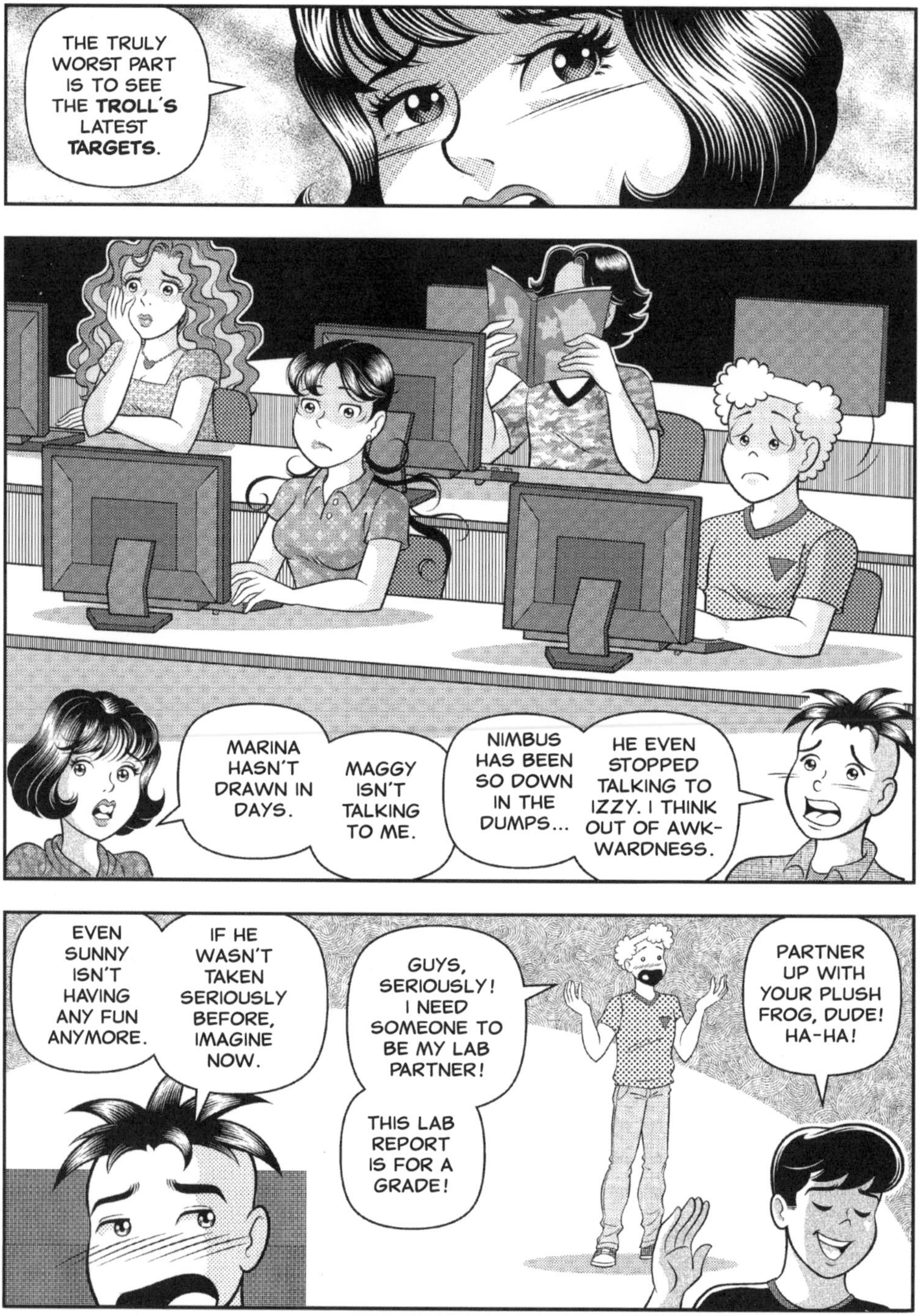
THE TRULY WORST PART IS TO SEE THE **TROLL'S** LATEST **TARGETS**.
MARINA HASN'T DRAWN IN DAYS.
MAGGY ISN'T TALKING TO ME.
NIMBUS HAS BEEN SO DOWN IN THE DUMPS...
HE EVEN STOPPED TALKING TO IZZY. I THINK OUT OF AWK-WARDNESS.
EVEN SUNNY ISN'T HAVING ANY FUN ANYMORE.
IF HE WASN'T TAKEN SERIOUSLY BEFORE, IMAGINE NOW.
GUYS, SERIOUSLY! I NEED SOMEONE TO BE MY LAB PARTNER!
THIS LAB REPORT IS FOR A GRADE!
PARTNER UP WITH YOUR PLUSH FROG, DUDE! HA-HA!

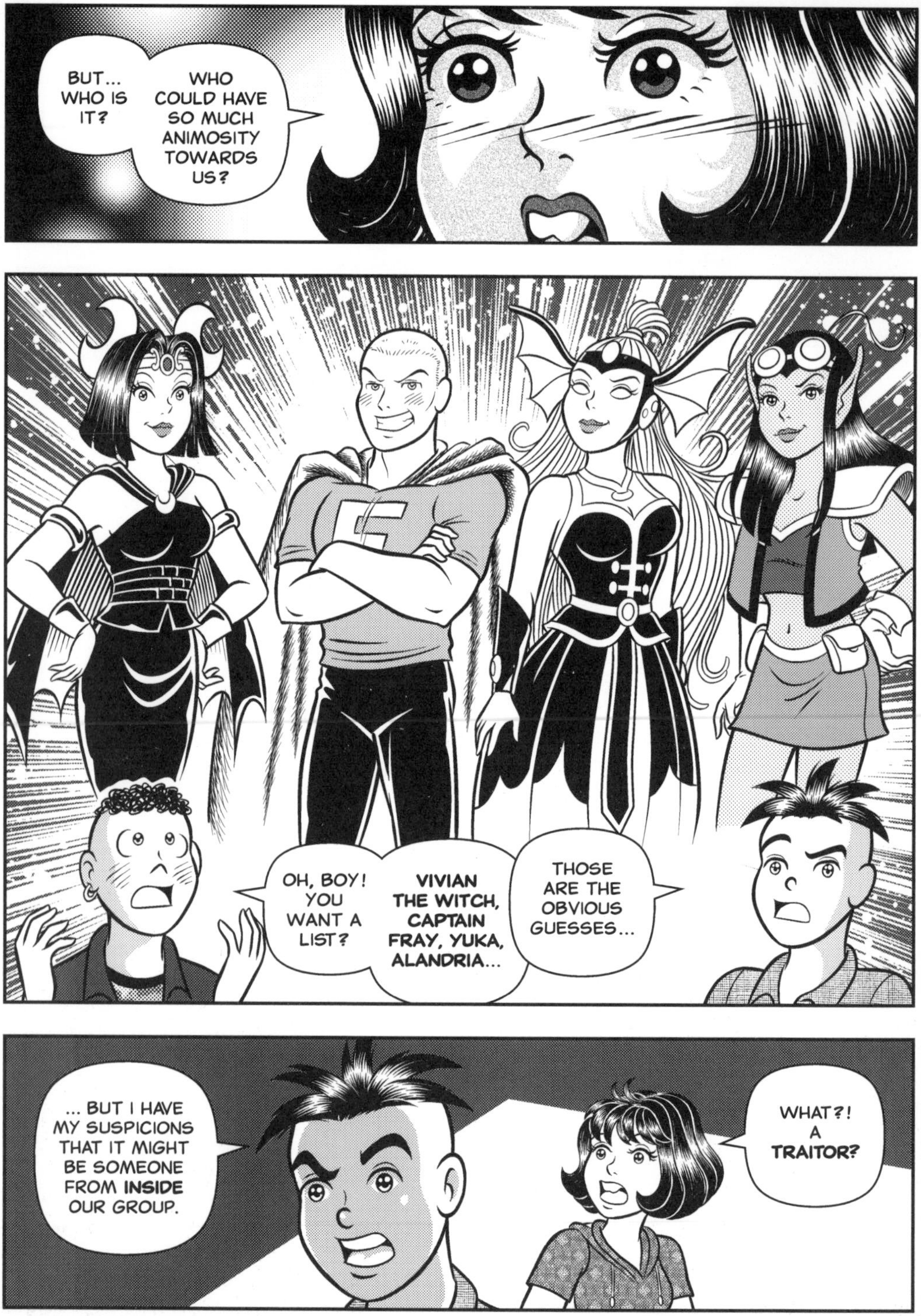
BUT... WHO IS IT?
WHO COULD HAVE SO MUCH ANIMOSITY TOWARDS US?
OH, BOY! YOU WANT A LIST?
VIVIAN THE WITCH, CAPTAIN FRAY, YUKA, ALANDRIA...
THOSE ARE THE OBVIOUS GUESSES...
... BUT I HAVE MY SUSPICIONS THAT IT MIGHT BE SOMEONE FROM INSIDE OUR GROUP.
WHAT?! A TRAITOR?

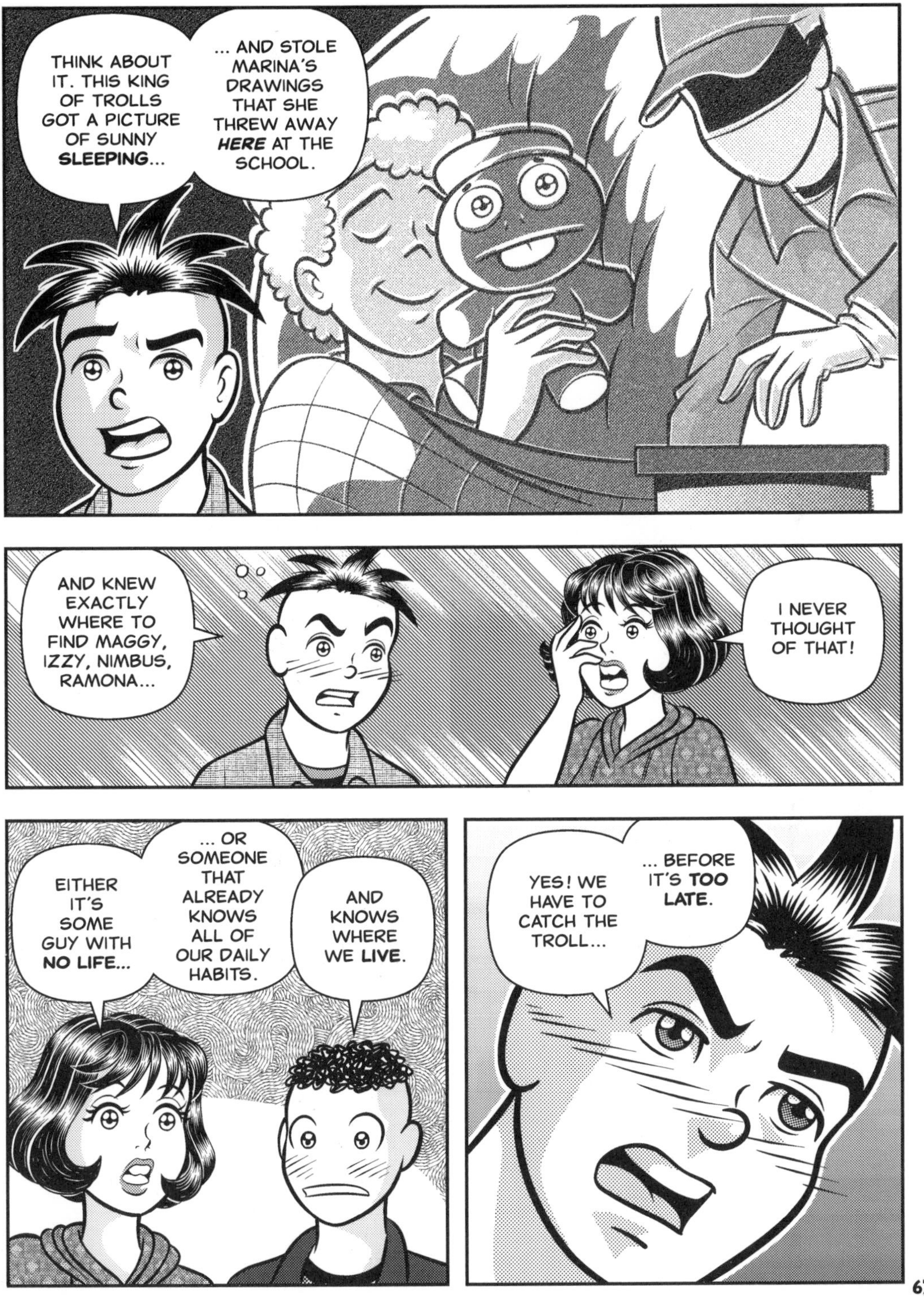
THINK ABOUT IT. THIS KING OF TROLLS GOT A PICTURE OF SUNNY **SLEEPING**...
... AND STOLE MARINA'S DRAWINGS THAT SHE THREW AWAY ***HERE*** AT THE SCHOOL.
AND KNEW EXACTLY WHERE TO FIND MAGGY, IZZY, NIMBUS, RAMONA...
I NEVER THOUGHT OF THAT!
EITHER IT'S SOME GUY WITH **NO LIFE**...
... OR SOMEONE THAT ALREADY KNOWS ALL OF OUR DAILY HABITS.
AND KNOWS WHERE WE **LIVE**.
YES! WE HAVE TO CATCH THE TROLL...
... BEFORE IT'S **TOO LATE**.

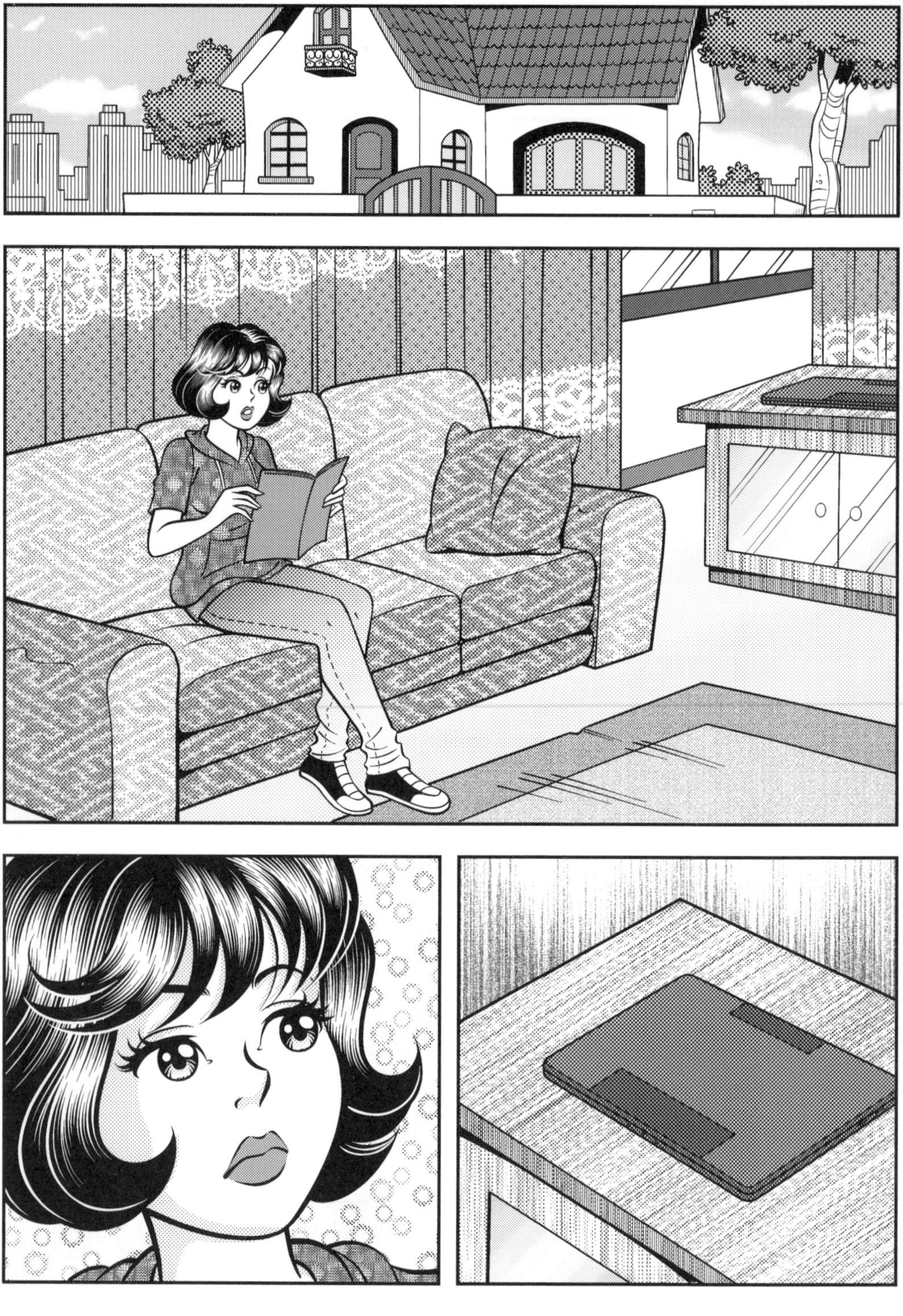

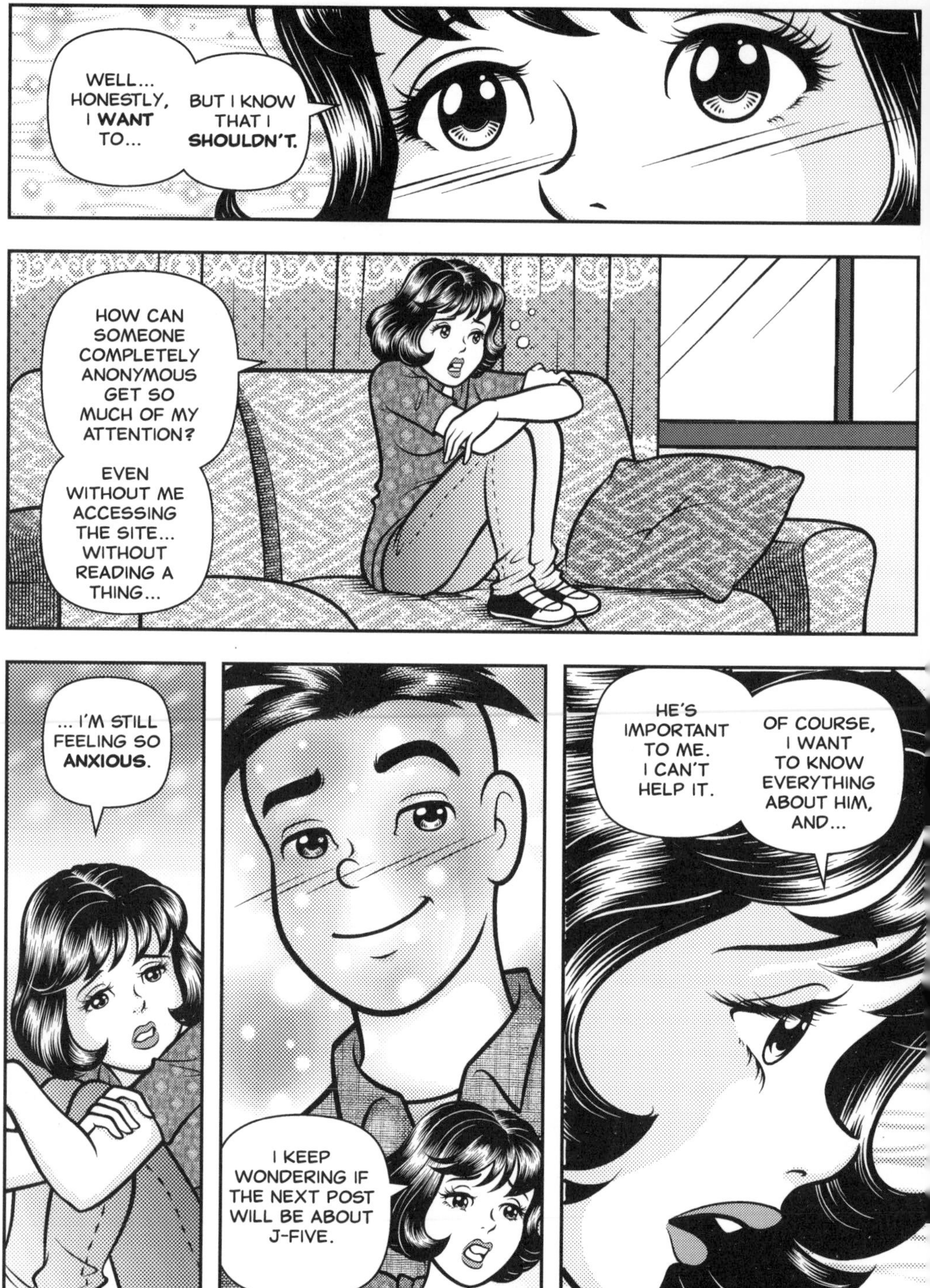

WELL... HONESTLY, I **WANT** TO...
BUT I KNOW THAT I **SHOULDN'T.**
HOW CAN SOMEONE COMPLETELY ANONYMOUS GET SO MUCH OF MY ATTENTION?
EVEN WITHOUT ME ACCESSING THE SITE... WITHOUT READING A THING...
... I'M STILL FEELING SO **ANXIOUS**.
I KEEP WONDERING IF THE NEXT POST WILL BE ABOUT J-FIVE.
HE'S IMPORTANT TO ME. I CAN'T HELP IT.
OF COURSE, I WANT TO KNOW EVERYTHING ABOUT HIM, AND...

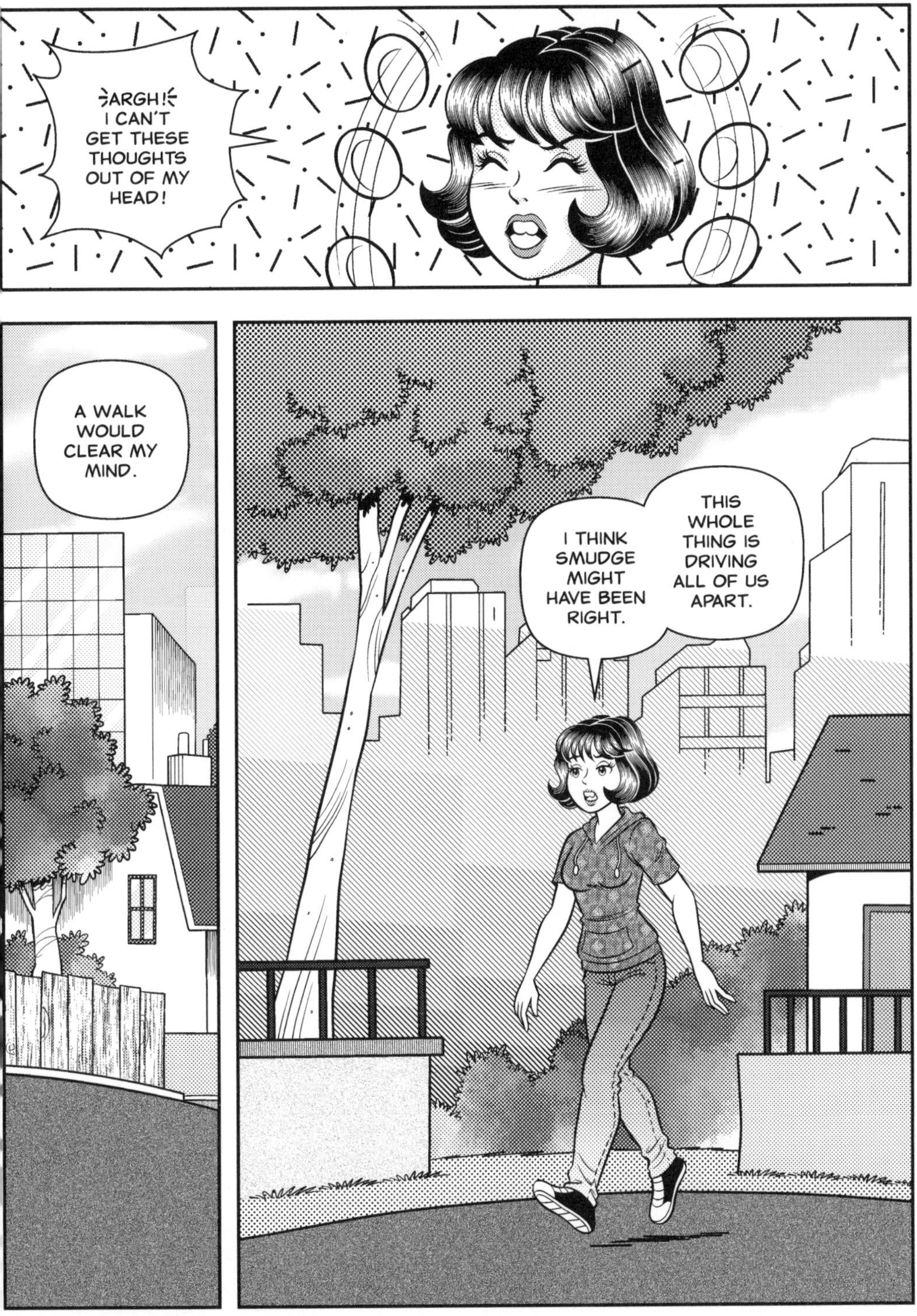
ARGH! I CAN'T GET THESE THOUGHTS OUT OF MY HEAD!
A WALK WOULD CLEAR MY MIND.
I THINK SMUDGE MIGHT HAVE BEEN RIGHT.
THIS WHOLE THING IS DRIVING ALL OF US APART.

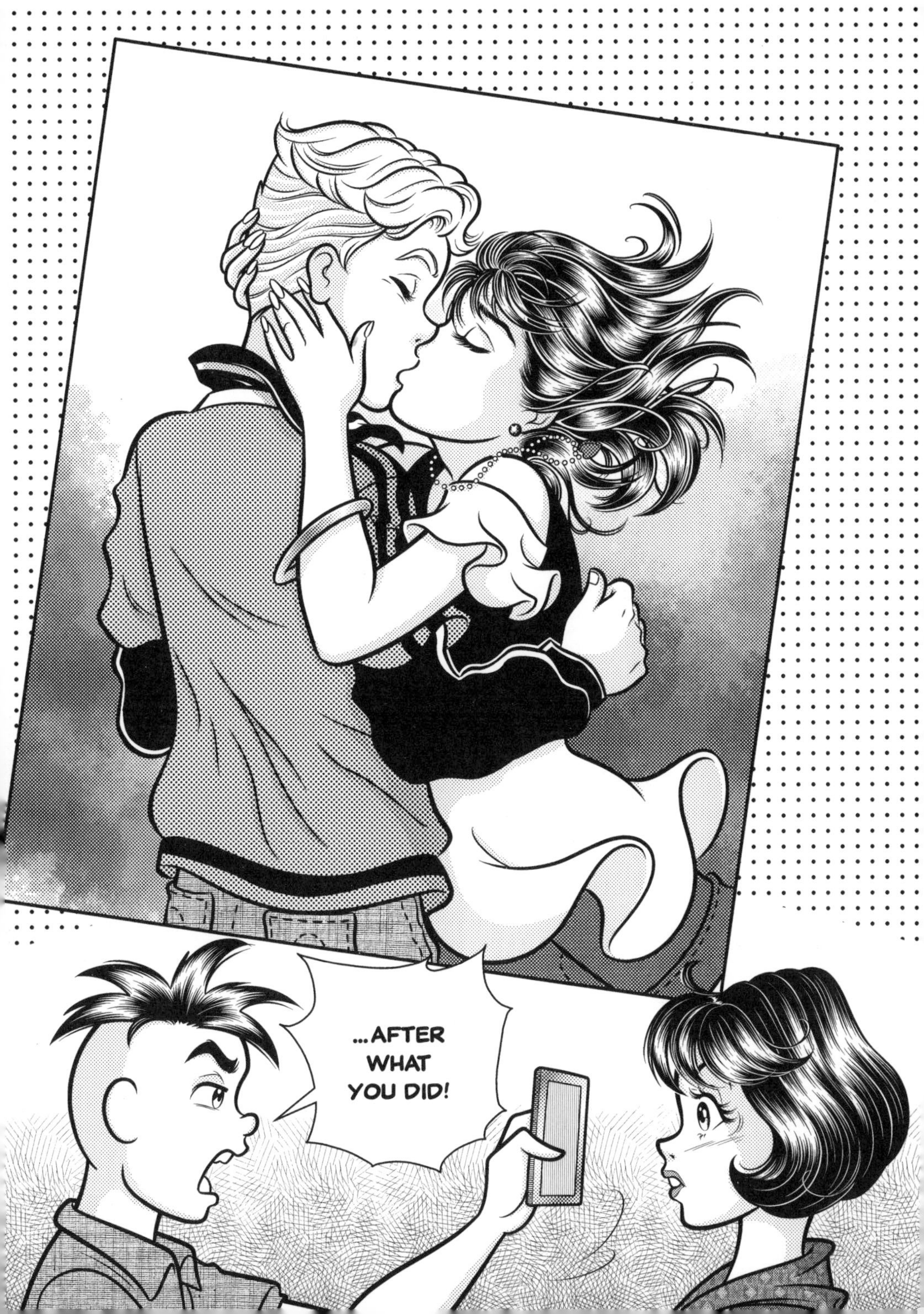
...AFTER WHAT YOU DID!

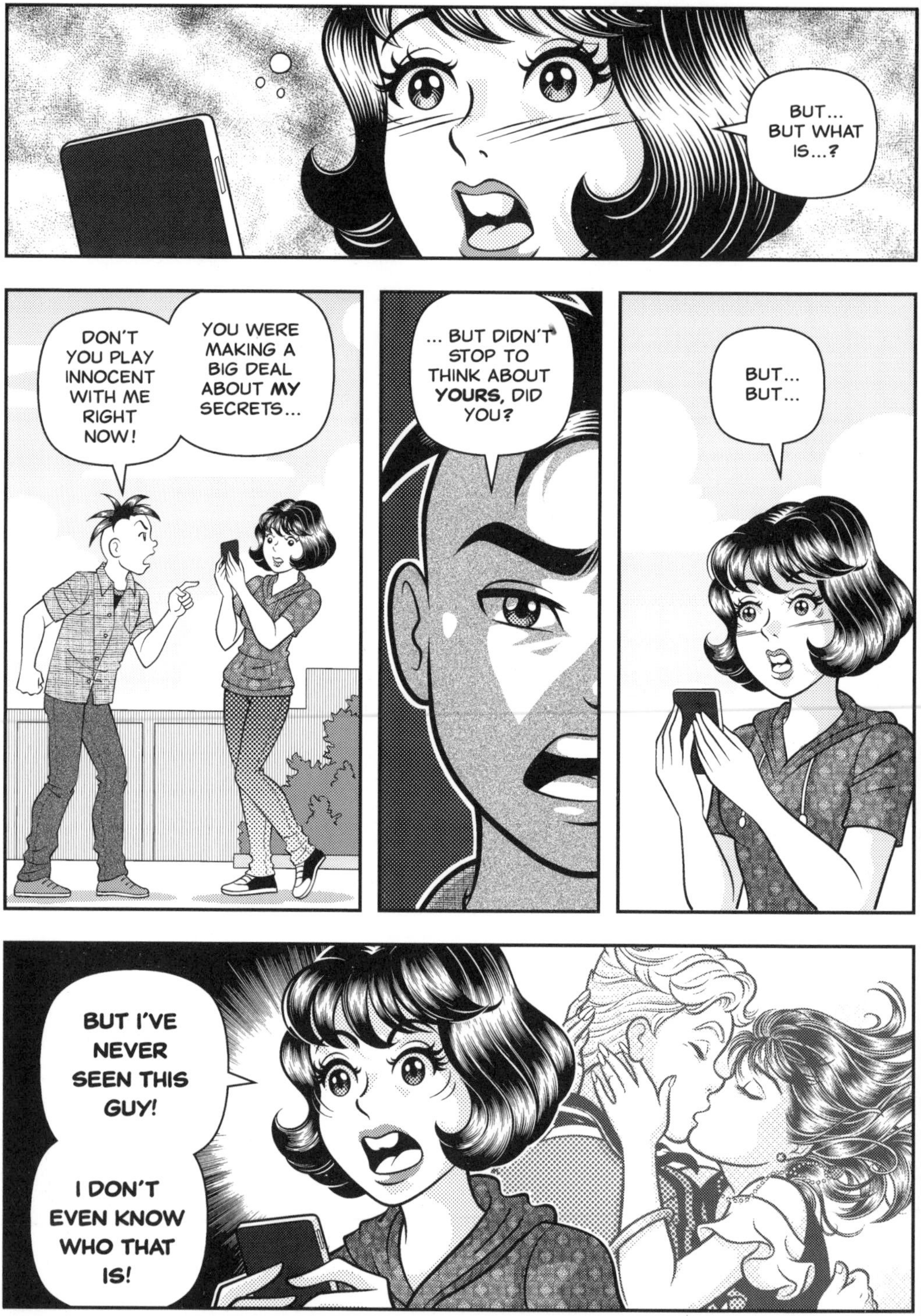
BUT... BUT WHAT IS...?
DON'T YOU PLAY INNOCENT WITH ME RIGHT NOW!
YOU WERE MAKING A BIG DEAL ABOUT MY SECRETS...
... BUT DIDN'T STOP TO THINK ABOUT YOURS, DID YOU?
BUT... BUT...
BUT I'VE NEVER SEEN THIS GUY!
I DON'T EVEN KNOW WHO THAT IS!

83

THE NEW POSTS ARE ALWAYS IN THE AFTERNOON AND AT NIGHT.

THAT MUST MEAN THAT HE'S BUSY IN THE MORNING. LIKE ME.

HE MUST BE A **STUDENT**!

WHO WOULD GO TO ALL THESE LENGTHS JUST TO FABRICATE GOSSIP AND--

HONEY! ONE OF YOUR GIRLFRIENDS IS HERE, WANTING TO TALK TO YOU!

ꜣUGH!ꜣ I DON'T WANT TO SEE **ANYONE**!

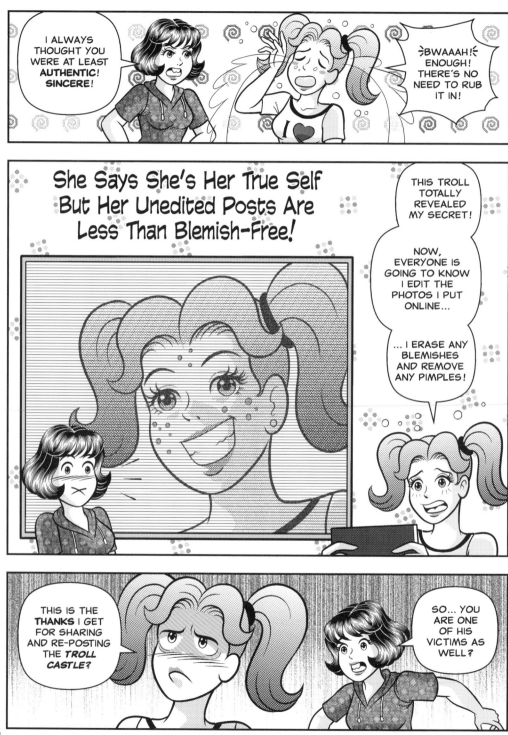

YOU DON'T EVEN HAVE TO SAY ANYTHING. I ALREADY KNOW WHAT IT'S ABOUT.

AND I DON'T OWE AN EXPLANATION TO ANYONE.

DO YOU KNOW HOW SERIOUS THIS IS, MISSY?!

BAH! YOU THINK YOU CAN THREATEN ME?

MY REPUTATION ALREADY WENT DOWN THE DRAIN. IT CAN'T GET ANY WORSE THAN THAT!

LEAVE ME ALONE! I HAVE TO FIND REPLACEMENTS FOR MY ENTIRE WARDROBE.

Dresses Better Than You, Richer Than You, But Still Uses Knock-Off Clothing. We Have the Proof!

Deoore

WELL, TO BE FAIR, EVERY-ONE KNOWS **THAT BRAND** SHOULDN'T HAVE SO MANY LETTERS

EXCUSE ME, NO ONE ASKED YOUR OPINION, MISS!

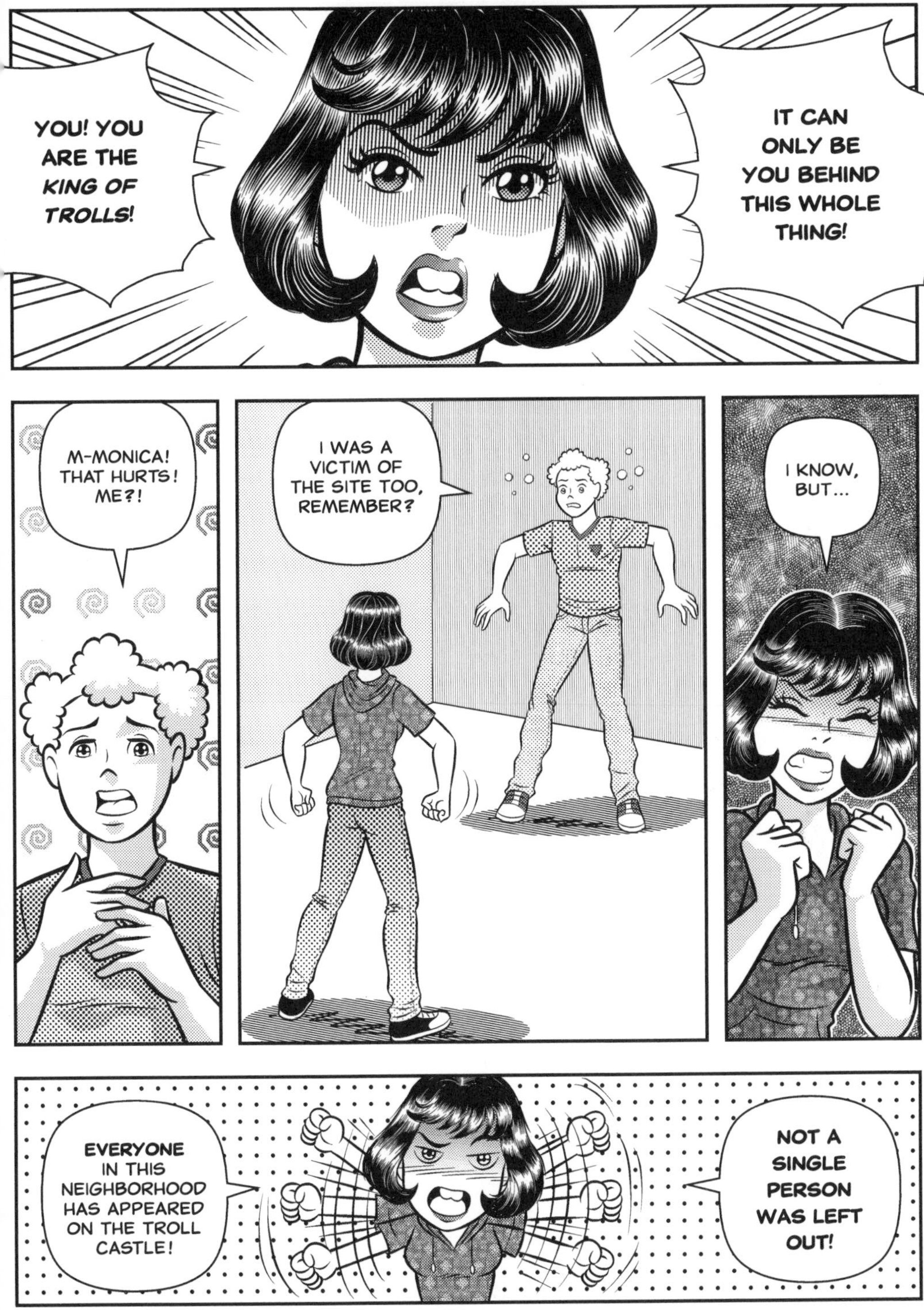
YOU! YOU ARE THE *KING OF TROLLS!*
IT CAN ONLY BE YOU BEHIND THIS WHOLE THING!
M-MONICA! THAT HURTS! ME?!
I WAS A VICTIM OF THE SITE TOO, REMEMBER?
I KNOW, BUT...
EVERYONE IN THIS NEIGHBORHOOD HAS APPEARED ON THE TROLL CASTLE!
NOT A SINGLE PERSON WAS LEFT OUT!

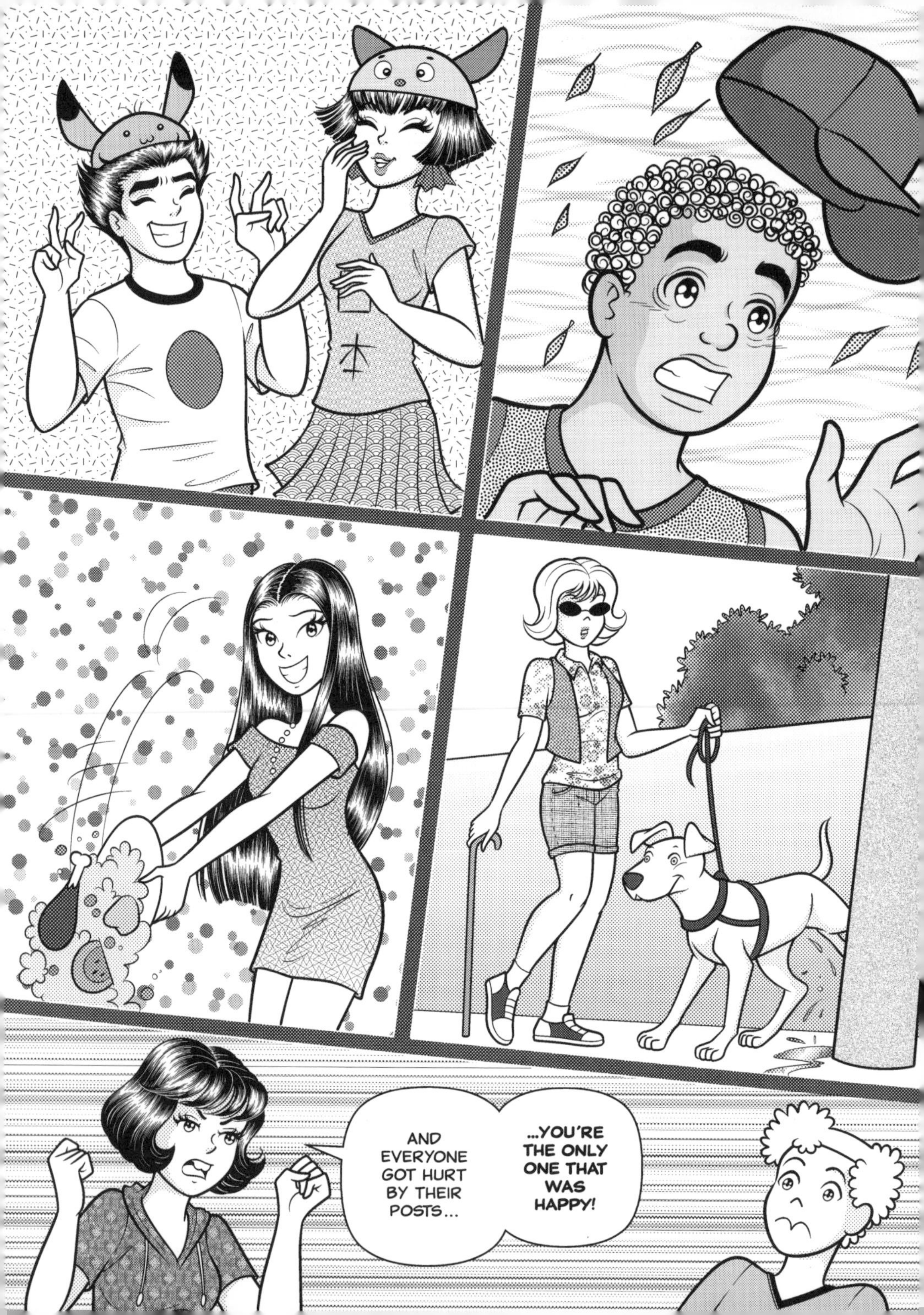
AND EVERYONE GOT HURT BY THEIR POSTS...
...YOU'RE THE ONLY ONE THAT WAS HAPPY!

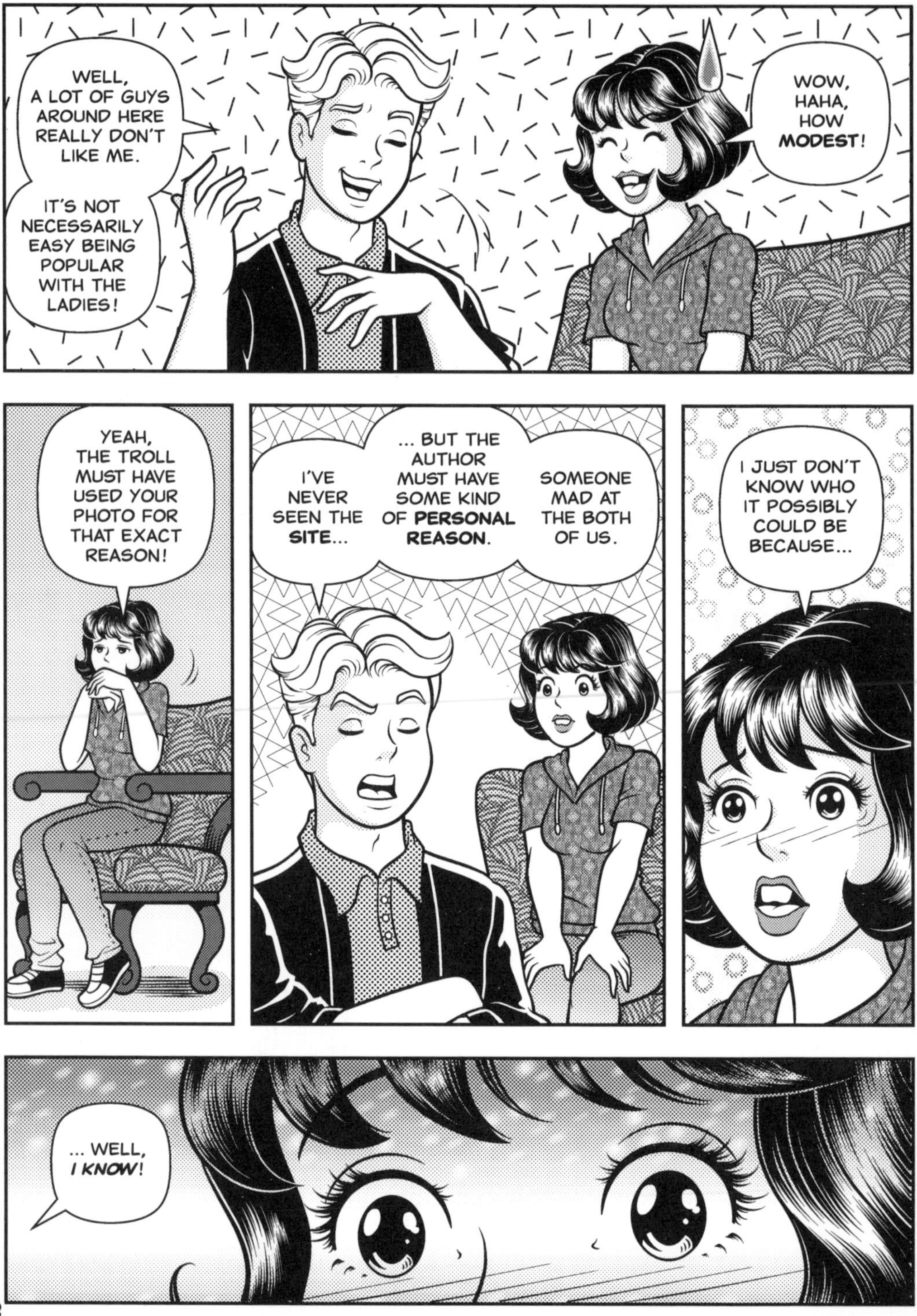
WELL, A LOT OF GUYS AROUND HERE REALLY DON'T LIKE ME.
IT'S NOT NECESSARILY EASY BEING POPULAR WITH THE LADIES!
WOW, HAHA, HOW **MODEST**!
YEAH, THE TROLL MUST HAVE USED YOUR PHOTO FOR THAT EXACT REASON!
I'VE NEVER SEEN THE **SITE**...
... BUT THE AUTHOR MUST HAVE SOME KIND OF **PERSONAL REASON**.
SOMEONE MAD AT THE BOTH OF US.
I JUST DON'T KNOW WHO IT POSSIBLY COULD BE BECAUSE...
... WELL, ***I KNOW***!

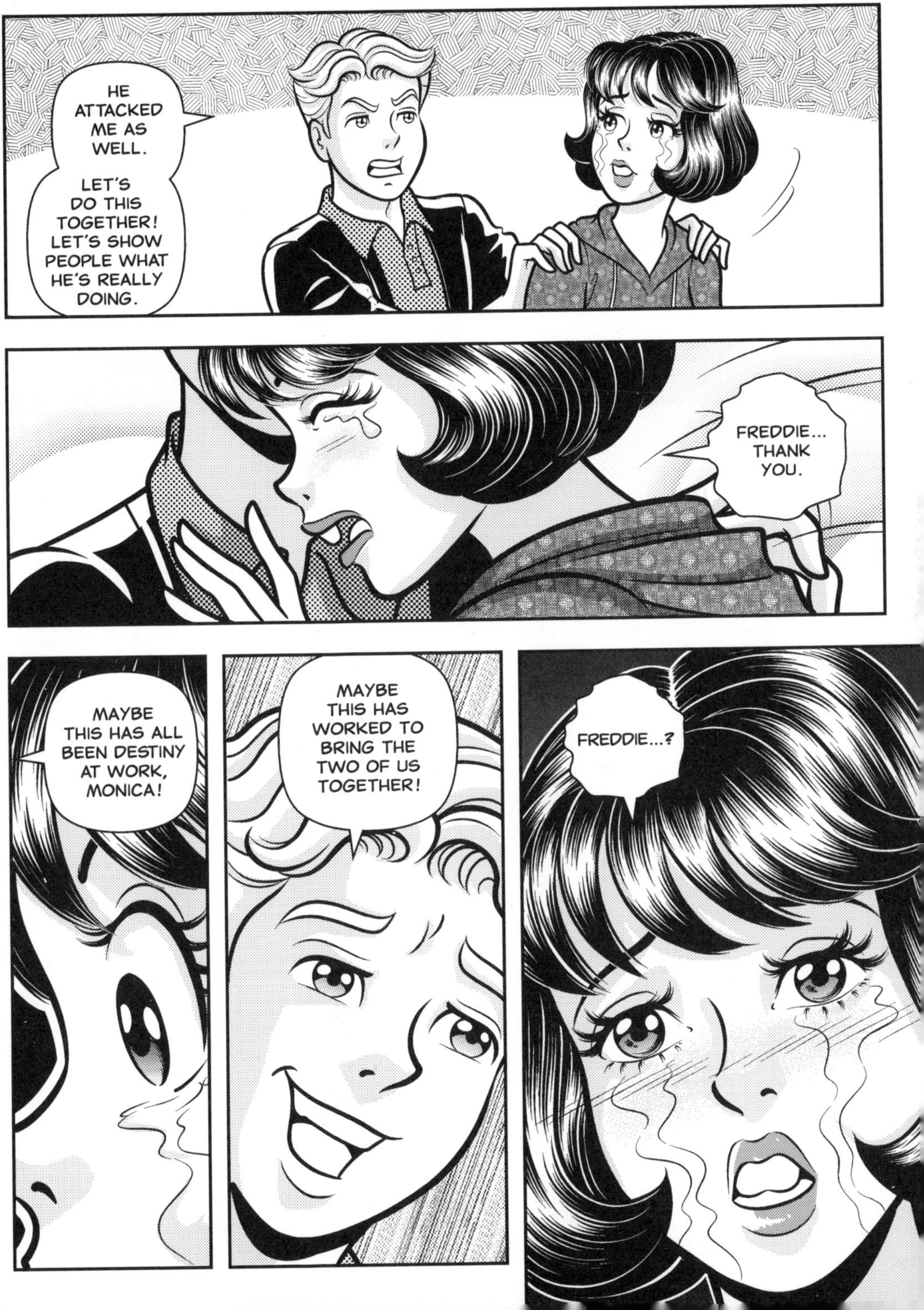
HE ATTACKED ME AS WELL.
LET'S DO THIS TOGETHER! LET'S SHOW PEOPLE WHAT HE'S REALLY DOING.
FREDDIE... THANK YOU.
MAYBE THIS HAS ALL BEEN DESTINY AT WORK, MONICA!
MAYBE THIS HAS WORKED TO BRING THE TWO OF US TOGETHER!
FREDDIE...?

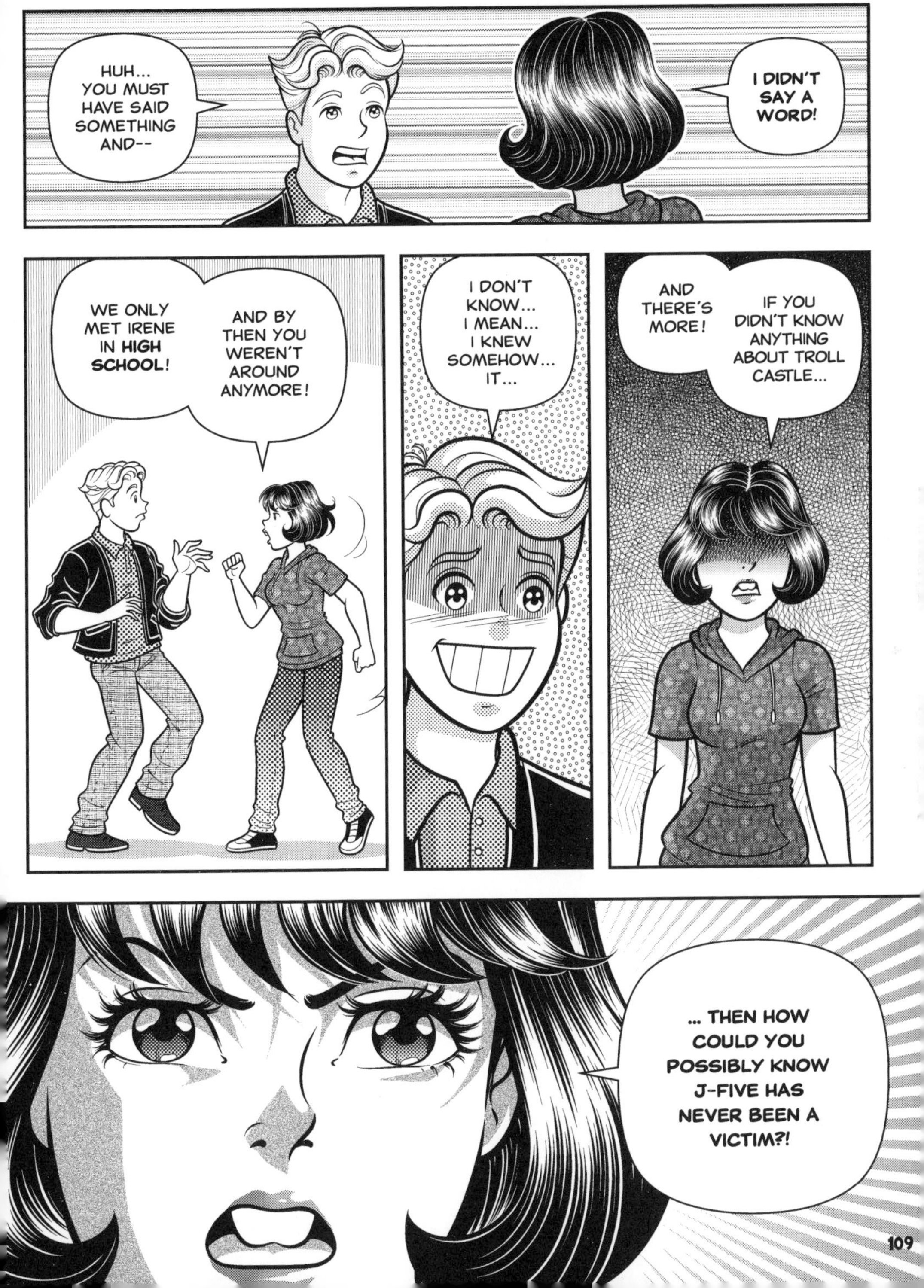

HUH... YOU MUST HAVE SAID SOMETHING AND--
I DIDN'T SAY A WORD!
WE ONLY MET IRENE IN **HIGH SCHOOL**!
AND BY THEN YOU WEREN'T AROUND ANYMORE!
I DON'T KNOW... I MEAN... I KNEW SOMEHOW... IT...
AND THERE'S MORE!
IF YOU DIDN'T KNOW ANYTHING ABOUT TROLL CASTLE...
... THEN HOW COULD YOU POSSIBLY KNOW J-FIVE HAS NEVER BEEN A VICTIM?!

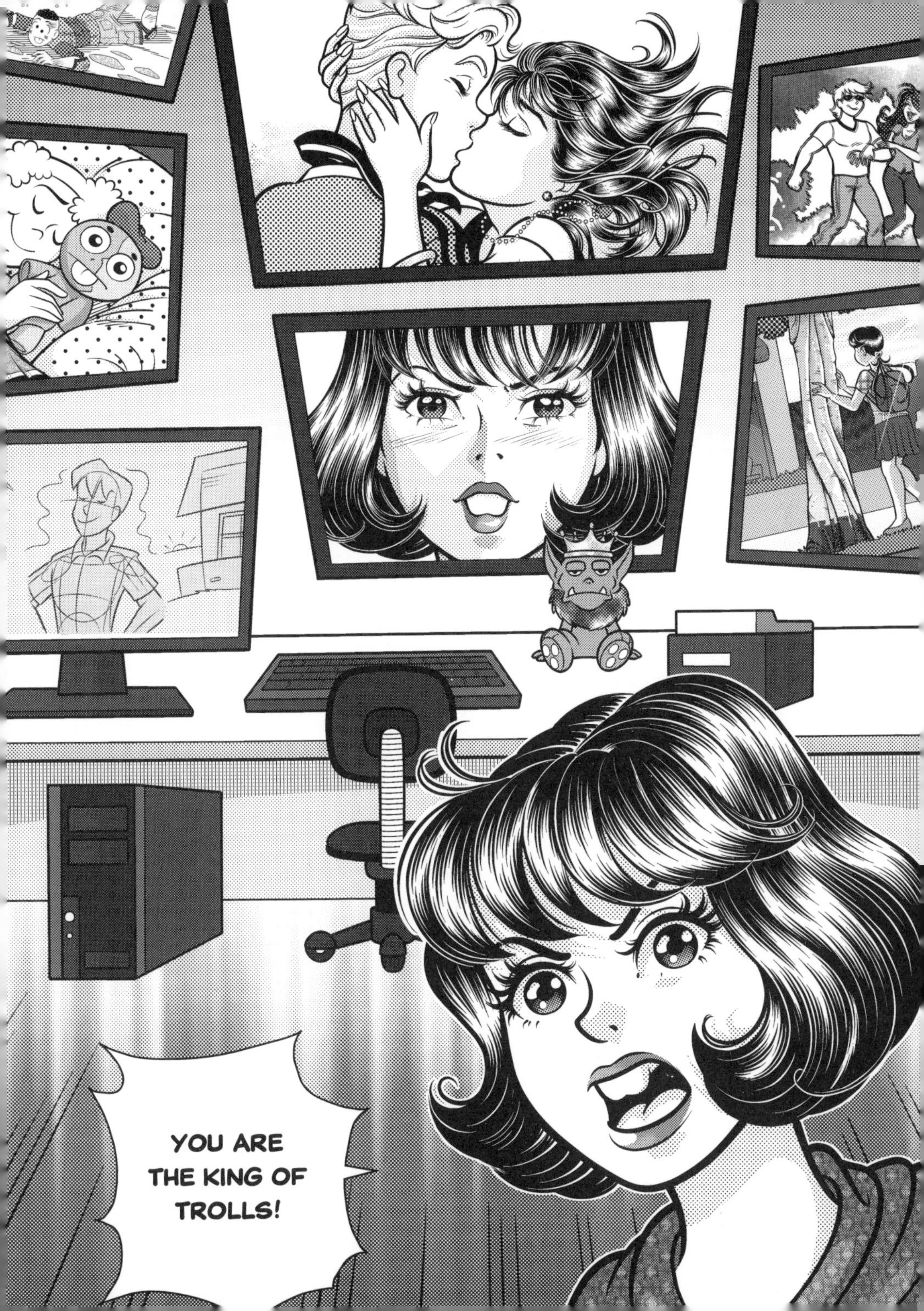
YOU ARE
THE KING OF
TROLLS!

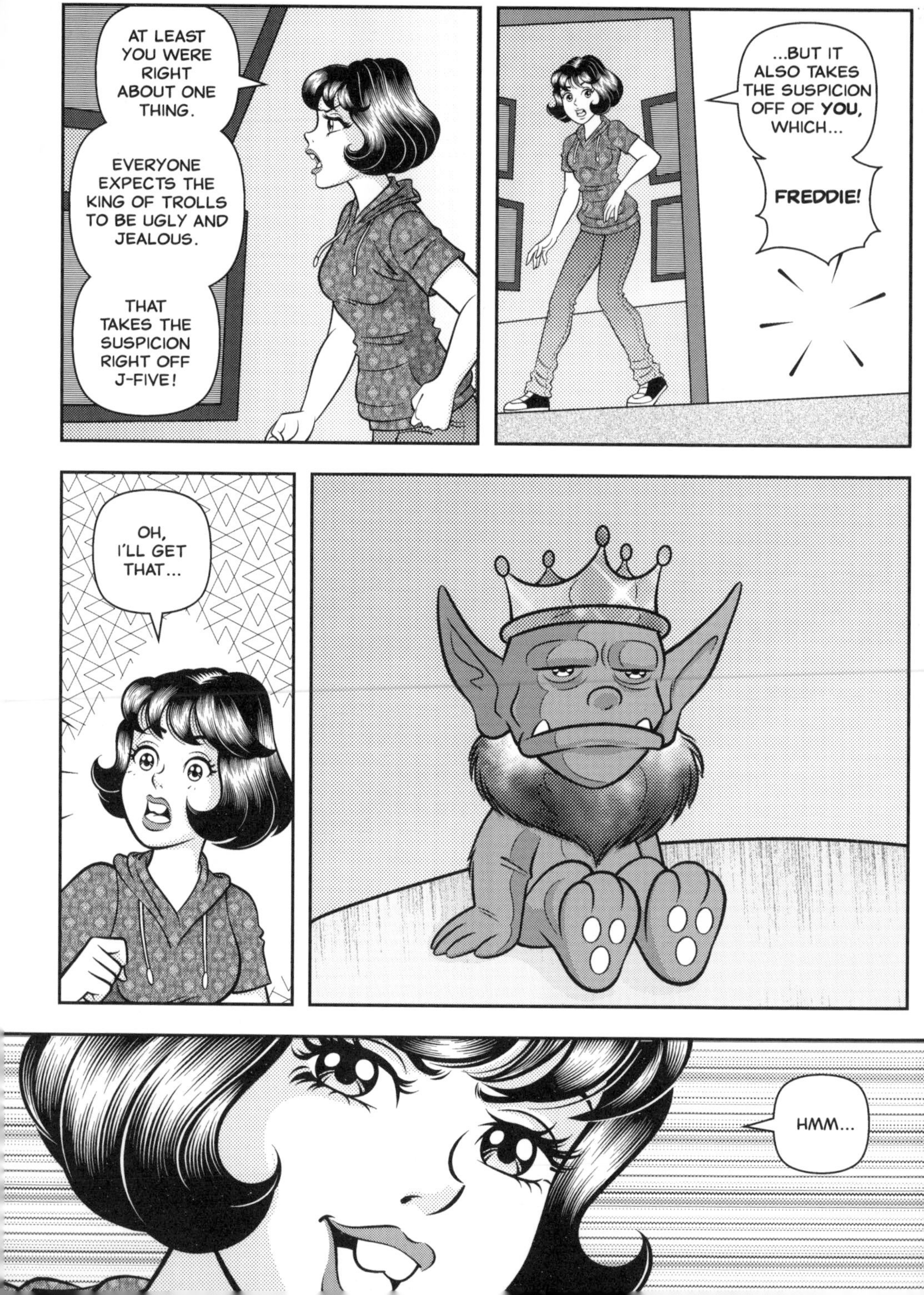
AT LEAST YOU WERE RIGHT ABOUT ONE THING.
EVERYONE EXPECTS THE KING OF TROLLS TO BE UGLY AND JEALOUS.
THAT TAKES THE SUSPICION RIGHT OFF J-FIVE!
...BUT IT ALSO TAKES THE SUSPICION OFF OF **YOU,** WHICH...
FREDDIE!
OH, I'LL GET THAT...
HMM...

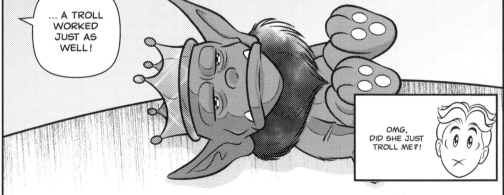

119

122

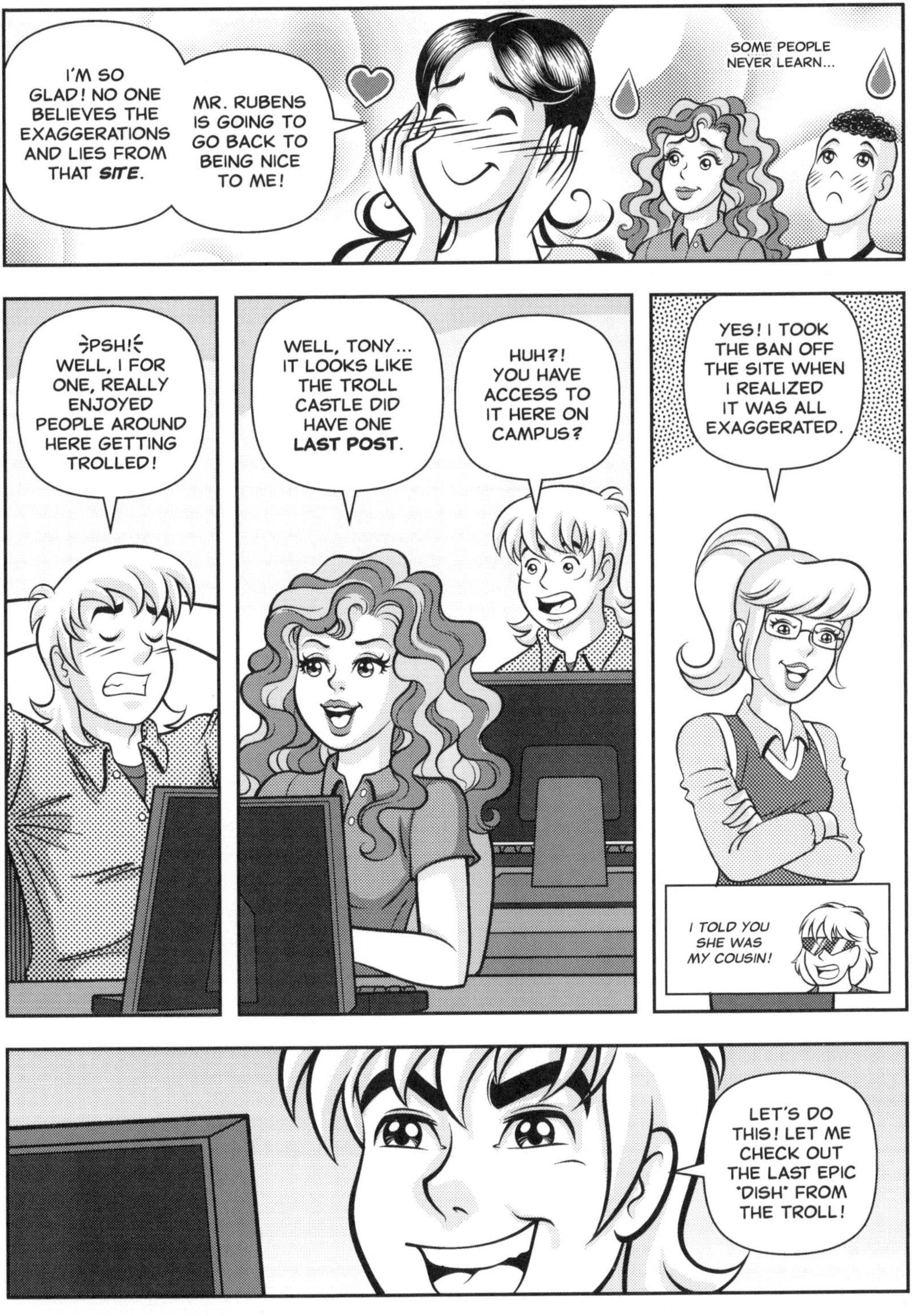
I'M SO GLAD! NO ONE BELIEVES THE EXAGGERATIONS AND LIES FROM THAT SITE.
MR. RUBENS IS GOING TO GO BACK TO BEING NICE TO ME!
SOME PEOPLE NEVER LEARN...
PSH!
WELL, I FOR ONE, REALLY ENJOYED PEOPLE AROUND HERE GETTING TROLLED!
WELL, TONY... IT LOOKS LIKE THE TROLL CASTLE DID HAVE ONE LAST POST.
HUH?! YOU HAVE ACCESS TO IT HERE ON CAMPUS?
YES! I TOOK THE BAN OFF THE SITE WHEN I REALIZED IT WAS ALL EXAGGERATED.
I TOLD YOU SHE WAS MY COUSIN!
LET'S DO THIS! LET ME CHECK OUT THE LAST EPIC "DISH" FROM THE TROLL!

In the dark corners of the internet, evil eyes are lurking ready to troll.

And trolls can emerge where you least expect it.

Enemies of reason and peace, determined to create confusion, spread discord, and diminish self-confidence… this new villain should be called out and confronted.

But this is not a common fight, as we are acustomed to. This fight starts with our strategic escape. Because, at the first sign of an ounce of indifference, the Troll's power is diminished, the Troll dies. The Troll loses power when they aren't confronted or responded to. We don't always have the patience or energy to ignore the tricks of a troll. We are not always immune to our own weakness of wanting to speak out against trolling. But time shows that we are the ones losing when we confront them. Trolls lack ethics, morals, and limits. They are amoral.

If we enter on the same playing field as the trolls, we lower our standards, and end up pawns in their own game. Avoid this. Soften your reactions.

Walk away. It isn't cowardly; it's bold.

Contradicting your natural defense mechanisms demonstrates courage, force, and resolution. It helps "control" the beast.

Push it to the deep dark depths of the Internet.

Mauricio
Mauricio de Sousa

charmZchat

Welcome to MONICA ADVENTURES #3 "Who's Saying Nasty Things About Me… Online?!" from those social media savvy types at Charmz, the Papercutz imprint devoted to romantic and fun graphic novels.

Back in MONICA ADVENTURES #1, we talked about Monica and her creator, Mauricio de Sousa. We explained that the character of Moncia started as a young girl taking charge of her neighborhood along with her friends (and frenemies) Maggy, Smudge, and "Jimmy" J-Five.

In this graphic novel series, Monica is a teenager in high school, it seems that not everyone she knew when she was younger may have grown up at the same speed intellectually. When we grow up, some-times we lose touch with old classmates and people who might go to different schools. Do you have any old friends you may have lost touch with? While this volume focuses on the dangers (or entertainment if you ask Denise) of social media, and care should be taken online to protect your privacy, one of the great things about social media is the ability to re-connect with old friends. We feel that same way when enjoying a comic or graphic novel, even thought we realize these are ficticious characters, we still feel like we are connecting with dear old friends.

Monica is willing to break the internet to keep her friends happy and safe. She is a powerful friend not just in strength, but in her determination to problem solve and figure out the true identity of the Troll King who is causing all her friends harm. Heroic, everyday stories like these are the most relatable. Other strong protagonists in our Charmz line are just as heroic in their own way. Middle schooler Chloe Blin needs to stand up to bullies and face her fears as she starts a stressful internship in CHLOE #1. Amy Von Brandt, who goes to a private school, must cope as her mom is ready to date after the death of her father. AMY'S DIARY #1 is full of drama, as well as her trying to find her place in the world, if she even belongs to this world—the jury is still out on that. And then there's Cherry Costello who has to put on a brave face to face her four new step-sisters, not all of them happy to have her, as she and her chocolatier dad move-in in SWEETIES #1. Lastly, Crimson Volania Mulch has to piece herself together, literally, as she wakes up as a patchwork girl in a cemetary in STITCHED #1 . All of these young people have their own challenges to brave and their own important support systems in place made up of friends, family, and even teachers, coaches, or supervisors.

So, yes, all of these characters are fictional, but that doesn't mean we can't learn from them, does it?

STAY IN TOUCH!

EMAIL: whitman@papercutz.com
WEB: Papercutz.com
TWITTER: @papercutzgn
INSTAGRAM: @papercutzgn
FACEBOOK: PAPERCUTZGRAPHICNOVELS
FANMAIL: Charmz, 160 Broadway,
           Suite 700, East Wing,
           New York, NY 10038

MORE GRAPHIC NOVELS AVAILABLE FROM charmz™

STITCHED
The First Day of the Rest of Her Life
charmz

STITCHED #1
"THE FIRST DAY OF THE REST OF HER LIFE"

STITCHED
MARIAH McCOURT · AARON ALEXOVICH
Love in the Time of Assumption
charmz

STITCHED #2
"LOVE IN THE TIME OF ASSUMPTION"

GFFs
charmz

G.F.F.s #1
"MY HEART LIES IN THE 90s"

GFFs
GHOST FRIENDS FOREVER
WITCHES GET THINGS DONE
charmz

G.F.F.s #2
"WITCHES GET THINGS DONE"

Ana
COSMIC RACE
THE RACE BEGINS
charmz

ANA AND THE COSMIC RACE #1
"THE RACE BEGINS"

Chloe
The New Girl

CHLOE #1
"THE NEW GIRL"

Chloe
The Queen of High School
charmz

CHLOE #2 "THE QUEEN OF HIGH SCHOOL"

Chloe
Frenemies
charmz

CHLOE #3
"FRENEMIES"

Chloe
Rainy Day
charmz

CHLOE #4
"RAINY DAY"

Chloe
Carnival Party
charmz

CHLOE #5
"CARNIVAL PARTY"

PATRICIA LYFOUNG
The Scarlet Rose
charmz

SCARLET ROSE #1

PATRICIA LYFOUNG
The Scarlet Rose
I'll Go Where You Go

SCARLET ROSE #2

PATRICIA LYFOUNG
The Scarlet Rose
I Think I Love You

SCARLET ROSE #3

PATRICIA LYFOUNG
The Scarlet Rose

SCARLET ROSE #4

PATRICIA LYFOUNG
The Scarlet Rose

SCARLET ROSE #5

Monica

MONICA ADVENTURES #1

Monica
We Fought Each Other as Kids... Now We're in Love?!

MONICA ADVENTURES #2

Monica
Adventures
Who's Saying Nasty Things About Me...Online?!

MONICA ADVENTURES #3

Monica
Adventures
Should I Say Yes... to Nick Hope?

MONICA ADVENTURES #4

Monica

MONICA ADVENTURES #5

Amy's Diary
Space Alien... Almost?

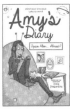

AMY'S DIARY #1

Amy's Diary
The World's Upside Down

AMY'S DIARY #2

Amy's Diary
Moving On

AMY'S DIARY #3

Sweeties

SWEETIES #1

Sweeties
SUMMER
COCO

SWEETIES #2

SEE MORE AT PAPERCUTZ.COM

NOOOOOOOPE...
You got it all backwards! You can't read this comic if you start from here. I understand that the original Japanese manga is read in the traditional "right to left" style... But I had a little conversation with Mauricio and he let us keep our stories the way we are accustomed to - from left to right. Let's agree that even though these comics have a manga style that we respect very much, there is still much of the original Monica's Gang in them too...
Enjoy!
Monica.
"IT ALL STARTED TODAY AFTER CLASS..."
HA-HA! HA-HA!
AW "J", YOU ARE SO ADORABLE!
WHAT?
GULP! UM... I SAID "THAT LAST ONE WAS HORRIBLE"!
GOOD THINGS OR BAD?
REALLY?!
ALRIGHTY!